TICKNOR

SHEILA HETI

ANANSI

Published in 2005 by
House of Anansi Press Inc.
110 Spadina Avenue, Suite 801
Toronto, ON, M5V 2K4
Tel. 416.363.4343
Fax 416.363.1017
www.anansi.ca

Distributed in Canada by
Publishers Group Canada
250A Carlton Street
Toronto, ON M5A 2L1
Toll free tel. 1.800.747.8147

09 08 07 06 05   1 2 3 4 5

Library and Archives Canada Cataloguing in Publication Data

Heti, Sheila, 1976–
Ticknor / Sheila Heti.

ISBN 0-88784-191-0

I. Title.

PS8565.E853T43 2005   C813'.6   C2005-900646-3

Cover and text design: Bill Douglas at The Bang
Author photograph: Janet Bailey

Canada Council
for the Arts
Conseil des Arts
du Canada

ONTARIO ARTS COUNCIL
CONSEIL DES ARTS DE L'ONTARIO

We acknowledge for their financial support of our publishing program the Canada Council for the Arts, the Ontario Arts Council, and the Government of Canada through the Book Publishing Industry Development Program (BPIDP).

The author acknowledges the financial support of the Ontario Arts Council, the Ontario Arts Council's Chalmers Program, and the Canada Council for the Arts. And heartfelt gratitude to Carl Wilson.

Printed and bound in Canada

TICKNOR

I

THERE WERE NO BOOKS when I was a boy. Books were hardly accessible, yet there were some books. That is why I did not develop literary taste. I read what I found and it was for fun. You read mostly for idle pleasure. I did not read for fun, nor was I cultivating my mind. I cannot imagine cultivating anything as a young boy. It is not my fault if I was not an erudite boy. Other boys had books and other boys had libraries. No, the whole country lacked books then. Comparatively few were published here, and they were borrowed with difficulty. There is no possible way I could have read good books. It was for pleasure that I read them, when I finally did. Today you read books. Yes, today I read books but there were no books when I was a boy, and I do not read books the way that other men read books. My taste, then, was juvenile. But you were like all the other boys. Sometimes you went to the library, but there was no library until much later. When I went to the library I would read the books that amused me. I had no taste

when I was young. I had no books. It is not my fault if
I read the lighter books, and that when I found them I
read them with a juvenile fever. But you would read
with no fever at all. You read on cool spring days, once
there were books in Mr. Shaw's library. I read the
books of the kind-hearted Mr. Shaw because I was
bright, and because he let me. This allowed me no
social pleasure. He would return from a fashionable
watering place and share with me his "loafing time"
while I was trying to read. His particular doctrine did
me no favours. He did little to nourish my mind. I was
given the lightest literature while the other boys
drowned in a great sea of social amusement. So long as
I could endure the task, I passed long hours on cool
spring days idly reading in the library of Mr. Shaw to
the unhappy exclusion of whatever perfectly youthful
enjoyment the other boys sought. The day came when
I made an attempt to quit Mr. Shaw's company, but he
said he would prefer it if I did not. I dropped my hand
from the windowsill and returned to my desk. Although
I can read, I do not read as well as I would like to.
Those hours influenced my literary tastes.

Some men love wild animals. I am not one of those
men. Animals have no place in my life, and I am not the
type to say he prefers animals to people. That is not
the sort of logic I agree with at all. I do not agree with
the logic of animal-loving men. Nor are you the sort of
man who would get along well with animal-loving

women. There is something stunted about those kinds of women. I am not a stunted man, though I am a difficult man. You have no difficulty with other people, and you cannot rightly say that your first and second loves were books. There was a woman I loved more than books, but now she is gone. I was not a favourite of girls, and I am still not favoured among women. You loved first a drunk, second a woman who was deformed in the face. I have only ever loved hopeless women, which is surely what has kept me from the highest circles. It's all that would have been necessary to find myself in the warm glow of the dinner table at the Prescotts'. To have only had a woman you could show off would have put you in the proper place. I tried not to love the women I loved. Now I only want to be quite simple and childlike with some dear woman, with no code of morals, yet I fear it's too late. Few people feel a real and deep passion more than once in a life. Perhaps you will never again love in the same true way, or find a human being who is such perfect rest to you.

It will take me a while to get there. You will get there soon enough. Getting somewhere always involves more effort than the effort of getting there is worth. Of course, there is nothing to be done about it. No one is eagerly awaiting you now. Your arrival is not anticipated with any great longing. Other men must hurry. If I am late it will mean nothing to anyone. You cannot be going anywhere with the thought that you are not wanted there. But it is the only way I can. There are friends of yours who eagerly await you now, and you will of course be late. I'm sorry I'm late. So sorry I'm late. You know how difficult it is to travel. You know how long these winding roads take. So sorry I'm late. Has everything already started? Is there nothing more left to this evening? I started out, and I was certain the supper hadn't begun. If only I had left the house on time. If I had just begun my journey when I first put on my coat and not stopped to write out the letter that was in my mind before I forgot it. I threw out the letter anyway. Had I left the house one minute earlier I would have caught the streetcar as it was moving away, or if the pie had been ready sooner, or if I had not made a pie at all, when you told me not to. The neighbours arranged for a party last night, so I had to sleep with the rubber earplugs in and woke up with a headache. I know you don't care. They never mind when I am late. There should be no rush in getting there. No, don't rush to get anywhere. Everyone will know it if you have rushed, and if they know you have rushed they will not think highly of you once you arrive. But I am not a late man. I hate to be late. I was not brought up in that easy way. I am not the sort of man who can afford to arrive any later than perfectly on time. Perhaps being late is better than on time, for a man whose arrival is not eagerly anticipated. My manner would become, perhaps, a little freer and easier from continual prac-

tice. You must take yourself for better or worse, however it is. Please forgive me. You know how the streets
are. Haven't you heard what happened on the street?
Before you leave, you cannot know the state of the
streets. Enough about the streets. They are not thinking about you now. Forget about them and forget about
the streets. Sorry I'm late. So sorry I'm late. But these
days everyone is always late. I'm sorry if I didn't arrive
on time. I left with lots of time to spare, but you know
the streets. It is so hard to go earnestly into the streets.

It would be better had I stayed at home. If you had
stayed home, how much better you would have felt.
This is not a night to be out in the streets. Not for an
old man. I am not quite so old. You had a mother but
your mother is dead. When mother died, she just made
up her mind and did it. She said she had nothing to live
for, then reached out her hand to touch me. She
missed. I was standing too far. I moved close to pull the
blanket over her head, and went to call the doctor into
the room. What was I to do? I stayed by him as he told
me all his plans, the usual rites to be taken care of. He
left to write out the certificate while I turned to look
at the blanket, adjusted it with one hand and played
with the lacy edge, then dropped it and left, shutting
the door behind me. It is that the street is so dark,
which makes the walking so terrible. There are many
gloomy nights and always more, and you are not at
home for enough of them. But I am home almost every

night. The invitations you receive come rarely, and the
ones that come you disdain. No, it would be terrible
at home. Not as lively as at the Prescotts'. They are a
lovely couple. They are the only couple you love. You
love them and yet you wish to be at home on a night
when you have nothing in particular to do. Besides, the
streets aren't so dark, and at the Prescotts' they will
warm your pie. Go now. You have only fifteen blocks
and already you are stalling. But it is not the darkness
of the night that bothers me. It's that I hate the rain.
The transition will be easy once you perceive it for
yourself. But it's not there and I fear it won't come. Go
home if you want. You said you would bring the pie. It
is not the night for writing letters. Forget the letters.
You rarely write letters and the ones you send are often
lost. Your life is in one sense more and more retired.
You write one or two household friends whenever they
happen to be out of Boston. It is not a correspondence
that is being preserved. I saw parts of it from ten or
twelve years ago, when I was visiting outside of Boston,
and I am sure my correspondence is being preserved.
Your correspondence is not preserved by your friends
and it is not preserved by the critics. In the preceding
two months you have written only three persons.
The two or three friends who live outside of Boston
hardly know what to make of your letters. They say you
shouldn't write them at all. Writing by the light injures
your eye. Chopping wood brings relief, but this is not

always understood. You should not speak so cruelly of the Prescotts. They are your closest friends and your only friends.

So sorry, Mrs. Abb_ng_on. I'm so sorry for not replying to your kind letter earlier. In any case, my days have been filled with nuisances. So sorry, Mrs. Abb_ng_on, for not replying to your letter at once. My days are filled with chores. You know they are like the days of everyone we know. You know everyone's days are filled with the worst sorts of interruptions. We laugh about the interruptions, but please forgive me. Are you well, Mrs. Abb_ng_on? I hope you are enjoying the fur coat you had fitted. I hope your husband sees how you are enjoying the fur. It has been very cold as winter approaches, and no doubt the fur will come in handy. Tonight I was at the Prescotts'. Tonight the Prescotts invited me for dinner and I went there with a pie. You know the Prescotts — they are my very best friends. It has been so long since I received such a nice letter, and though I did not reply at once, I have been thinking of you constantly. I thought of you often. I often thought of writing, but you know the interruptions of life. Mrs. Abb_ng_on, I hope you don't hate me now that it has taken me so many months to reply to your kindest of letters. It is very cold in the streets, and it is impossible to go anywhere in Boston without wasting half your day in getting there. People are cold and cruel and nobody comes with the streetcar when you need it. The stores are lined with advertisements and you cannot look anywhere without being sold something. There are fewer and fewer days with sun, and many people are currently out of work. Perhaps you received my last two letters? If your husband's factory has closed, I'm terribly sorry. Perhaps my last few letters were lost. I assume my correspondence was lost in the mail, but please don't hold it against me. This happens to me on a regular basis. You are one of the dearest women I know, Mrs. Abb_ng_on. It was terrible walking through the streets on a cold night like tonight. I was on my way to have supper with the Prescotts. Perhaps you remember Mrs. Prescott? She wore the red feather at the literary lunch. I'm sure you remember her. Please forgive the delay in my reply. There is a charming shady walk by the house where I live. When you visit Boston next perhaps you will come and see me, and we will take this walk. I often walk before dinner, and I love companionship at that time of the night. It is at that time of the night when I am most in need of friends. The drives are less agreeable but the walks still have their charms. Everything around here is familiar and dear to me and reminds me of all the days of my childhood. Perhaps you will visit me, when next you come to Boston. Please come to Boston, Mrs. Abb_ng_on. I hope to see you in Boston, but I suggest you wait until winter has passed.

He lived with his mother and father and I lived all alone. Even when he was only living with his mother I was living all alone. There is nothing to envy about a grown man living with his mother and father, but then his family has always been close. And the homes — even his opulent apartments were unlike the simple apartments of his friends. Everyone would have liked to live in them. Often you slept there, so you are closer than most, though you found out that others did too. You pretended not to want to be a part, but they could tell you wanted to be a part; everyone did anyway, you found that out, if you didn't know it already. And they like your company, so it's not an intrusion. They like me as an outsider and friend, and I have always been at a familiar distance. Even with the grandmother. But you cannot envy the grandmother, who cannot remember a thing, though the ease she knew must have existed as some sort of comfort in her senility. There couldn't have been the same anxiety in senility that one would normally expect from an old woman. Still, you had good homes too, if not in the same way. Your father would sooner lose all his money than occupy a summer house, though it was always the wish of the family. You can't be the son of someone else's family. You would go home and there were secrets you didn't know about. The fights they had, you don't know about those, the mother shouting that she hopes she gets cancer. If you knew their fights better maybe you wouldn't envy their homes. Or maybe you would envy more. Why shouldn't the worst be equally appealing? You were welcomed in, but in the discomforting way of close families — at the end of the night they were never sad enough to see you go. They would wave you out cheerfully and close the door. There's no use feeling lonely about that loving sort of family, when they wanted to share it with you, some. You can't look to your childhood now and think you should have spent more time with his mother and father and the rest of them. Even if you had, you would not have become a better man or written any books of history. If your family now seems to you not what you thought it was as a child, still your childhood sits well with you, even if there was a greater fragility to it than you realized. But their intimacy is a kind of comfort I wouldn't have wanted, no. How could I have lived like that in a tight family with open arms to the outside world? Now I am alone and otherwise it wouldn't have been so easy. The house had nothing pretentious about it, though the furniture was rare. The walls were rich. Sometimes large parties were given, and seasonal dinners with many friends and games. Nights of dinners to which I was sometimes invited. Not so often; they had many friends. Everyone was privileged to enjoy them, felt the privilege of being there. The first house they occupied was on Tremont Street and the next on Summer Street. Both have now been pulled down to make room for the heavy bricks and granite blocks demanded by commerce. He used to talk about his childhood in their first home in Boston, a mansion, really, moving from New York as a two-year-old and the empty stairwells and the ghostly corners. Home was always a word of peculiar import to him, and any interference with his old habits and associations in relation to it became most unwelcome after his mother and father died. What's left is a more modern house with children and a wife. The simplicity of their lives is not to be mistaken, though rich and substantial. There's no desperation to recapture something of the past, and no trace of loneliness can be seen on his face at their suppers. Even at the house after we all came back from the cemetery, everyone wanted to be seen as a closer friend of the family, and help in a more significant way, looking still to the family in the kindest, most innocent of ways for some slightly exasperated remark about the other guests. How no one else deserved to be there as much. But that idea could not be sustained, not with a family in mourning. You were and still are privileged to enjoy it, and it is all attractive, quiet, gentle, and warmhearted. You are an intimate friend. You are known as an intimate friend by the entire widely branched family, and you could not be more a part of something that was as sought after as the home and household of the Prescotts, even after the death of his father and mother, though not as much after that. So you bring the pie.

There is no reason for the rain to prevent you or the cold to prevent you. You have no excuses when you look to the weather, or to the quality of the night, or to the streetcar, though it is very slow. No one has been rude to you in the streets, so even that is not a reason to stay in tonight. Prescott has your admiration, and you have his as well. As a handsome boy he once executed a perfect tumble down a flight of stairs before a hallway filled with boys, and bounded up proudly on the bottom landing and smiled right at you. But I was absent on a journey from the beginning of December to March and did not see him once. During the whole of his trying period I did not see him, and when I returned, I entered his room uneasily, expecting him to curse me outright. But he was perfectly natural and very gay, and it was my manner and voice that were ashamed and fearful and morose. Soon we began talking in the old, common way. You talked as though in your absence there had been no absence, and he did not correct you. Perhaps he was grateful. He was perhaps more grateful than I, and it made the day easier. I was perhaps more grateful than he was for this artificial lightness, though perhaps he was really, and I was made more uneasy by it, though of course also comforted.

When you returned, there was no feeling left in him for you. He was curious about your several months in Europe and what your travels had been about, and he talked briefly of his own troubles, of the pain that had attacked him in the early winter and had been subsiding only slightly. You still think of that, but that does not mean he thinks of it every time he sees you. No, it's obvious he doesn't. Nothing is able to affect the natural flow of his feelings for a permanent time. Those who know him as one commonly knows a man may find these accounts of his private habits unexpected, even exaggerated; however, during the whole of his trying period he remained agreeable and gay and made no righteous show of the admirable virtues that everyone knew he possessed. The foundations of his character were laid deep. His correspondences at the time were at their best. I had believed friends were preserving mine, but in visits outside of Boston they showed me his. It wouldn't matter so much if it weren't for the fact that I made no copies. I don't care whether or not they're being preserved by acquaintances outside of Boston. When I send mail it is often lost — so most of my friends feel I lead an unprofitable life, but pardon or overlook it as a misfortune. Even tonight it will be no different. If you think your absence would make him particularly gloomy you are wrong, and you could as easily have stayed home as gone out. Do not visit for his sake. He has the pleasure of his family and whatever friends they might have invited. His equanimity and cheerfulness are invincible.

It was only after having returned from my journey of several months that I found everything changed, his

gatherings as much attended by those curious to meet
the son of William Hickling Prescott Sr., said to be
remarkable, as those who wanted to show themselves
off, young men and old from the academy and literary
circles. His parents had grown proud of the once-
solemn young man who overtook the study, then the
sitting room and the sleeping quarters of a maid who
was no longer needed, and it wasn't long before the
whole thing grew established in the mould that had
been set by his father, and soon after that he took for
himself the house on Beacon Street, not far off. The
entire time I was gone my eyes were set on home, and
it wasn't until I returned that I discovered what had
occurred. While I had acquired nothing, the glory of
his name was already all about him. Archbishop
Hughes publicly praised him for his judicious treat-
ment of the Catholics, and though two years previous
he had been known to only ten people in New York,
that number had grown to more than two hundred, and
there was not one day on his whole five-day visit to
New York to begin work on his *Ferdinand* that he did
not wake after noon, dine after ten, or fall into bed past
two, expending all his spirits and energy with his new
acquaintances and friends. He had thought, on setting
out, that it would be no more than five days of loafing
in New York, and clearing up some details with his
publisher before returning to Pepperell and plunging
into his pages. But five days were soon extended to

twelve as the invitations of more than two hundred people assailed him, so that when at last he returned to Boston he was too weary to begin his work straight away. Too pleased by the cordiality he had known and still feeling the blush of the many gratifying tributes, he was in no way equipped to approach his book, the excitement of the social world having been too great. *Five days should be the limit*, he put in a letter to Claire. *How could I then spend a season in London? I shall not try.* He vowed never again to exceed two or at most three days visiting a great American city, and made good this promise the rest of his life.

Returning from my journey I had known none of this, and expected none of this from the solitary boy who had been my friend. I saw him only once before he left for London and Paris for medical advice. Following his return home, many months went by and no note came. At last an envelope arrived. I was invited to visit the following evening, and all day I occupied my mind with errands to distract myself from the approaching fact of the night. I brushed my hair well and found a tie beneath my bed. I put on the tie and buttoned my vest. Then, circling in my mind the little intimacies we two would share, I made my way through the streets. When I arrived, the door opened to reveal not the quietness of Prescott and Claire, but a house filled to bursting with brass buttons, men who could, without effort, best me in every possible way. I moved toward a divan, sat and bent down to adjust the sock that had gathered at the bottom of my foot on the walk over. When I stood up again, I was as lost as a card that has blown from a deck. Not one man turned to face me; no woman smiled my way. I saw there was nothing I could say to Prescott that these men could not put better, and it was not nine o'clock before I moved into the night, avoiding Prescott as I went — my friend who had chosen upon my return to parade himself before me and display what wealth of stature he had acquired in my absence, shedding the skin we had both worn, that now only I wore. Coming onto the lawn, there was laughter and the ringing of glasses which I could hear from where I stood, and lit up in the window and arranged behind the curtains, a premonition of the whole of Prescott's life was laid clear before me like a carnival poster. Seeing that, there was no hope left in me that things would right themselves, and should any force try to stop these men from gathering and using all of their influence to lift each other into the highest ranks, no fewer than two dozen able-bodied men from that room on Beacon Street would raise their swords against it, preventing any merit from draining from their positions as the heads and treasurers of every society and association in the Union. After that, I still did see him, though not as much. You say you saw him almost as much, but you barely saw him at all, and when you did there was always a group. He would have liked me to sit closer but other people pushed in beside him and he didn't seem to care. Still, he would smile, and it was not as though our friendship was ruined. You claim a friendship. Well, it has been that way since we were boys. Such a recording of events would only be of transient interest to him, so I don't bring it up. No, you have never remarked on it. His disposition fared well; he could have been ruined, but he wasn't.

There was something you never did that you ought to have done, which is why it has turned out the way it has. I could not have known that I would never again be so much a part of something as sought after as the warmth of his household, but since the death of his mother and father, what has become of it? A modern home with a modern wife and children, none of the luxuries of Tremont Street, none of the furnishings of Summer Street. You went away and when you returned there was no feeling left in him for you. For the whole of his trying period I was gone, and though I knew I must write him, I could not. Then many months went by and I still had not sent it. Now it is too late. I don't believe he even thinks of that time anymore. When I left that winter his eye was excessively inflamed, very swollen, the cornea opaque and his power of vision almost completely lost. The whole system, in short, was very much disturbed, and the case had evidently become one of unusual severity. Still, he sat there talking.

We talked and he was curious about my coming travels in Europe and what they were to be about for me, but soon his mother was calling him to bed. He handed me a smile in apology, then went with her anyway. There was no desire in him to stay past our time. There used to be so many hours lost, enjoying each other and laughing, hours passed without our knowing it, but after that night I came to accept this new footing and did not ask for anything more. Of course, he never gave any sure sign that he had lost his genuine affection and was acting out of politeness or a sense of duty — always he denied having acted out of duty — yet before I left he asked only about my travels and did not speak about himself at all. Shortly after, he set to work on his history and found a wife to marry, and everything was as though the injury had never occurred, though he could only read for two or three hours of the day and only with assistance. You never assisted. He had friends who were less close than I who wanted to assist, but there was something in it I wanted no part of. Perhaps I should have seen it for what it was, like being invited back to the house after the funeral — perhaps everyone was only being helpful and kind. The entire family behaved politely towards me after I returned from my trip of December through March, but I still think that when his mother and father died it was not with love for me, and how could I be a comfort to Prescott when he already had the affection of Claire? I knew I was not as important as Claire, so returning after the funeral I just stood around, wanting to let him know I was there — standing there with everyone else rushing about. I am not good at those sorts of arrangements, pouring drinks or holding out a hand to a woman to help her from her chair; even sitting in the corner of the parlour with the men, smoking and talking in appropriate ways. I had nothing to say in the appropriate ways. I could not help out because I no longer knew the house, not as some of the others did, or what was needed, or what they might have wanted from me. Several times, though perhaps as few as one or two, he did give me a direct, tired look, but I didn't know what it meant, whether it was mostly incriminating or not. I cannot go to his house. I can tell he doesn't see inside me or even care to anymore. He avoids my eyes, even when he greets me, smiling. During the whole of that trying period you hardly saw him, but when you finally did — if it can be called seeing, in a room from which the light was almost entirely excluded — he asked the sorts of questions everyone asked when you returned. But about to come out with an answer, something always wore away in me and I could not tell it with enthusiasm. It was determined shortly after that he would spend the next six months with his grandfather, then visit London and Paris for medical advice. You only saw him once between your return home and the day he left for his grandfather's house, and as you groped your way across the room to take your place at his side, did he greet you with anything but good cheer, as though you were the patient and it was his place to comfort you — even though so severe was his pain, and so violent, that until the beginning of May, a period of seventeen weeks, he was unable to take the slightest step. The disease had affected the appearance of acute rheumatism, showing itself in the neck and large joints of his lower extremities, and twice after the first attack it recurred in his eye, accompanied each time by a total blindness. Five months were passed in this way, when he did not know if he would write again or ever read another book, but when I visited he asked only about my life. Even tonight he would welcome me in calmly, and if I did not know him well I would not be able to tell which eye caused him the trouble, and if I had not heard the stories of his remarkable spirit and perseverance in the face of such terrible health, I would not be able to sense a thing.

But no matter, I will still be as I am, whether I go and congratulate him on his book or not, and if I do not, another instance will have passed when I did not say a word, and if I do not show myself it will be too late. He will close up his face upon reading my note and pass it to Claire, who will toss it with a frown and a remark about what kind of man I really am, about how unfortunate are these childhood friends who stick around so long. *There's nothing to be done about it, Claire,*

I've known him all my life, even our fathers were friends.
Then back to the newspaper or whatever it is they do.
Everything should have been said already, so long ago,
and with an air of gracefulness and ease. That long
summer wore slowly away, not without anxiety on the
part of his family as to what might be the end of so
much suffering. But they had not foreseen that the
patient would end up in such a way, in such a light, in
the love of the press and his friends and the same warm
household that so many are privileged to enjoy, a complete glory shining down on him — which should not
have been unexpected since he was always perfectly
natural and gay, always talked unwillingly of his own
troubles, and was only awaiting a complete absence of several years, which at that time I was about to commence.

WHEN I HAD GONE that morning in a friendly way to enlist his opinion and help on my article, he was sitting at his desk writing and did not notice me there until I closed the door. Only then did he turn his head and tell me to sit, pulling a book from across his desk and giving it to me. I sat with it in my lap, across from him, not reading it with any attention of mind, looking up now and then over the top of it to see how he was occupied, but he was only sitting, working, not looking up, copying figures from one book into another. My eyes were wandering the walls. It was only later when the assistant returned and not when I arrived that Prescott shifted into a state of sudden activity, pushing a bell on his wall which drew into the room a boy who went at once to order the coal, and though his assistant was concerned that Prescott not do all the work on his own without a break and offered again and again to stay, Prescott was adamant. There must be a dozen Michael Sullivans on Broad Street, he reasoned. His assistant was to go and make certain the coal was received by his friend. He told him to take the five dollars he had pulled from his pocket to Mr. *O*'Sullivan — as he called him, teasingly — and gave the boy an order for a ton of coal that was to be delivered without delay to Michael Sullivan, Broad Street. I sat watching this exchange, waiting to see if Prescott would betray a lack of feeling, but he did nothing of the sort. He had been copying in his copy-book at one end of the desk while I was at the other, reading the book he had pushed into my hands, when twenty minutes later the young assistant still had not yet returned. Prescott got up, checking his watch, try-ing not to seem irritated, but when the young man hurried in and told him the reason for his delay, Prescott said nothing and went straight to his desk where scrap pieces of paper were kept and wrote out the order, no longer a bit upset. I pretended not to notice as the young man spoke quickly and confidential-ly about returning to his unemployed friend's room after having met the man accidentally on the street and finding, in the den where his friend lived, the man's wife and four children huddled under straw and chips of wood, trying to keep warm.

After ordering the coal with a decisiveness I could not imagine in myself, Prescott took the five dollars from his wallet and told his assistant to deliver it and not hurry back, but to stay with them until six, and then also to report to him whenever he encountered such a case, as he was rarely out in the streets himself but always wanted to know. Could the man be trusted not to spend the money on drink? The assistant assured him he could, and taking the bill he pulled the accounts book over and entered in his neat hand, *Charity, five dollars*, before heading off quickly with his coat and hat pulled on as the door shut behind him. Prescott had told him not to tell the young family where the money was from or else everyone from Broad Street would be at his door within half an hour, begging.

The assistant left and Prescott sat before me again. I felt grim and useless there. I had observed the whole exchange, saying nothing. Prescott had laboured the entire morning on the expenses and when I had come by he had sat me down, putting a book in my hands, claiming he wanted my opinion of it — though he never asked for it after that — while I waited with him as he finished his work, laying down row after row of numbers as I pretended to read. Of course, none of this was Prescott's work at all. He had a boy for that, but the boy was at lunch and Prescott would not encroach on the personal time of anyone he employed, this he was firm about. He would never allow anyone to work for him past the hours stipulated in the agreement.

The coal had just been ordered and there wasn't time to spare. After which it was my turn to go, I knew. We did not get to have our lunch together that day or the next. I had watched him pull the five dollar bill from his wallet, and after the others left, Prescott looked up at me from the hunched-over position he had resumed, altogether forgetting I was there, and apologized that he would not be able to stop work until six. I placed the book on his desk and made to leave, touching his shoulder, using all my strength of will to do it in a casual sort of way. It failed. *I would certainly go cautiously before the public in a completely new style of coat or hat, just as I would as a writer with a new style when I have already been praised for my last one*, he remarked, turning, yet he hadn't rustled the first leaf of my manuscript and it was clear now that he had no intention of coming to it or ever addressing it directly. Addison entered and went impatiently to Prescott's side while Prescott continued with his lecture, but I could not listen to Prescott when there beside him was Addison, who never remembered my name and was always pulling other men aside, making me want to disappear. I had spent too long labouring on that one article — not lengthy, but dense, and entirely about canals, a subject I knew and cared little about, but chose it because the field was relatively untouched, and then having discovered that the subject bored me, I continued on with it anyway. All of this made the writing of it even more strenuous, none of which could have meant anything to Addison, who was hanging off Prescott's arm, regarding me only impatiently and altogether refusing to leave. No, I would not be able to bring up with Prescott what had been in my head until Addison was gone, but Addison wouldn't leave and continued to rap insultingly on the desk. When at last he realized I was not about to go, he leaned over and whispered furiously into Prescott's ear. Prescott then stood and excused himself and the two of them went out, while I was left alone in his study at the wooden desk to wait some more, when all day and all week he had been expecting *me*, not Addison who had burst into his office without any notice at all, but who quickly became the first concern.

When it came to the point that I had been left standing a full half hour more, I snatched my hat and coat and left, unwilling to be humiliated a moment longer. I had not been so impressed with the speech Prescott had made. I had listened as the children passed by in the streets outside, making their way home from school. I had listened while waiting to bring up what had been in my mind so long and so significantly as he went on about tampering with style. But what had he even meant? I did not have the problems he did in the composition of articles. There is no style I need to maintain, but to follow the fundamental laws of writing is enough for me — clarity and what's familiar. I would not try to take on Prescott's style, a charm so individual that it was not permitted for any friend or critic to imitate it, and which would no more fit me than his coat or hat or shoes or gloves. I would not try such a thing, though I had attempted to show him my articles before, only to have him do as he'd just done, putting them aside for the following day, and by the following week forgetting that I had approached him with anything new. He would smile agreeably and place my papers behind him on a shelf as I watched them disappear among the piles of notes he had stacked there already. But there was nothing to be done. I left the house the long way and, passing the kitchen on my way out, took a long and steady look through the door at Claire's wide backside bent over in front of the pantry, keeping the sight of it for myself for the walk home. The shop windows were all boarded up. I would return home and make do with what I had in my room: the remains of a soup. And I would put into it what I could find — one potato, half an onion at the back of a drawer, the rings dried up, some barley and rice, a lot of salt. And it was not so terrible that I did not eat it all up, and even add in a carrot for a luxury, because carrots were so dear.

I have always wanted to reach out and grab her, though I never felt she and I had very much in common. One time when we were younger and Prescott was ill and had been put up in his bed for a week, and was so foul-mouthed that she was afraid of him whenever he called out to her — though, to forgive him, it was a time of much discomfort and I am not surprised it was so upsetting, what with his terror of not being able to see and never being able to continue his labours — he

called out to her as though she were merely a maidser-
vant and his own life ruined, as though she could not
understand a thing. It was at the end of that week, when
she had been absolutely battered by his calling out and
demands that she do all things for him herself, while he
let everything fall to the side, that I visited. Prescott
wouldn't see me, ill as he was, but he insisted that I stay
and instructed Claire to serve me my dinner down-
stairs, in the kitchen, and that I was not to worry about
being a burden for Claire, who had to make dinner anyway. Claire did not say a word so I feared she was
annoyed, but then she was famous for her patience with
all of Prescott's friends, and only once in the interven-
ing years did I hear a rumour of her rudely addressing
any man, when, at a literary dinner, Prescott was called
up to the stage to receive an award and Mr. Wh__ney
made a grand gesture from the audience to Prescott to
not forget Claire in his speech, offending Claire deeply.
But aside from that one time she was ever aiding in
counsel, reviving in troubles, and concealing of nothing
but her own sorrow, unless one acknowledges the per-
petual grimace which, it seems likely, she lost in the
privacy of her bedroom with Prescott, and there is
surely no limit to Prescott's endless demands there.

I sat politely at the counter as she was turned
away, continuing to cook while I sat watching and trying not to watch. But at the time the marriage was not
yet so old, and still I marvelled at my oldest friend's

good American wife, so modest and confiding and eco-
nomical, and how Prescott had so easily found himself
one when so recently he had been the baby of his
father's family. I dared not address her as I sat there,
trying not to stir. She continued to cook while I waited,
watching, occupied fully with her wild rump, which was
like a whole other being entirely; a lovely creature stuck
to her legs. There were only the meaty smells from
Claire's pots, the bubbling on the stove, and the sight of
her inviting behind, while I remained there, politely. I
would not have attempted anything on her. She was not
one of those flaunting, giggling, squandering, peevish,
fashion-hunting wives, and never once had Claire taken
more than a dutiful interest in me, allowing her hand to
be kissed or grasped, but no more. I knew her making
supper for me was only a way of appeasing Prescott,
and there was not a hint of anything but resoluteness in
it all. I knew this, yet I did not know it entirely, for
when she turned to approach with my potatoes and
meat I made a seductive face, licking my lips and grinning so that a jolt came to her, causing her nearly to
drop my plate, and she quickly hurried by me, up the
stairs, my supper still in her hand. I sat there in terror,
unable to think, while she was a long time in returning.
It is bad merchandise in any department of trade, Prescott
advised his friends on his wedding day, *to pay a premium
for other men's opinions. In matrimony, the man who selects
a wife for the applause or wonder of his neighbours is a fair*

way towards domestic bankruptcy. But at the time Claire was still a little beautiful and had not yet lost her figure, though she had long outgrown the coquettishness she had shown the world as a fiancée. Still, cooking for me that night, and as the minutes passed, I began to feel that, though turned away, she had some sense of the pleasure I was taking in watching her, and was aware, as I was, that this was the first time in all the years of her marriage to Prescott that she and I were alone together, now in the gently warming kitchen, and keeping herself turned so I could see her backside shift back and forth beneath her dress, I grew so moved at her acquiescence that tears came into my eyes, and come into my eyes today, just thinking of it. No woman has ever accommodated me so, and ashamed as I felt, burning all over, I was at that moment proud of nothing so much in America as our good American wives.

A TALENTED MAN PUTS all his understanding, all the sensitivity of his soul, into his work. My attitude towards work is obtuse and indifferent. Instead, I always liked the daughters who came to dine with their parents, or who came to clean the house. You think you were the only boy who liked the daughters? No, but if I had not liked the daughters so much I would have done anything for learning. I would have gone searching for books under the neighbourhood pines. It is not beyond belief; things were taking up my mind. But no, I do not blame the daughters. The pleasures I chose were short-lived. They expended my energy and spirits and still do. My interest in the daughters persists to this day and I take extreme care to keep up my correspondence with women, even if they often don't write, even if they surely won't visit. Letters were not foreign to me as a boy. I have no difficulty writing letters. The writing of letters is the thing I believe I do best. I have even been told that my letters are as good as some books.

Which books were mentioned? *Gulliver's Travels* for one. In which case, I try very hard not to let this skill deteriorate. I am very adept at talking to one person. That is the way I was raised. My parents were very polite, and what I lack in sophistication, I make up for in good breeding.

I return to you the vegetarian treatise with many thanks. Thank you for the treatise! I have read it over carefully and have given it a lot of thought. I do agree with the major points. I had never seen it spelled out in quite that way. For me it was a simple matter of pity before, but now I see it is as complex as a tree. Please tell me in your next letter how you find your health. Tell me how you find your health, when you write me next. I have given it a lot of thought and found it very convincing myself, especially the part about the vitamins. Thank you for sending it! I will pass on your notes to those friends of mine who are here at home.

My eye caught sight of your name this morning as I was riffling through the daily paper. How wonderful for you to have been published in such a respectable journal! I had no idea you had your father's talent. If you will remember, you once brought a poem to the house when you were only ten or eleven years old, and it was quite good. I still remember what it was about; there was a cat and a tree and a storm. I thought it depicted the troubles of adolescence and, to a lesser degree, the troubles in your family at the time. In any case, congratulations! I should like to go out with you some time and talk about your political ideas, to see what sort of a man you've become. If your father is not as proud as can be, I think it must only be because his eyesight is failing.

I cannot thank you enough for the third volume of your *Philip*, which you have had the kindness to send to me. I have been wondering what kind of shape you're in, but judging from this history's great success, I see you're better than I hoped. Having read only the first few chapters, I can tell you have done a great justice to your subject. I hope you are keeping an eye on our dear friend Prescott, whose success a fourth time around has been accompanied by a great roar from the national press. He and Claire are being as gracious as they can be, and have not yet held too many parties to celebrate. I have been begging every one of my friends to come and visit when the spring arrives, because I recently discovered some beautiful walks that I did not know existed, and which I cannot wait to explore. I hope that things continue this well for all of us. Your *Philip* makes me feel as if you're right here beside me, and reminds me of all our happy days at Pepperell. May you prosper and always continue to multiply the various pleasures of your life.

Mrs. M_ntague, would you be delighted to discover I have been worrying about you? Your son is doing two sculptures simultaneously and was amazed that I agreed to pose. He still stubbornly and silently eats breakfast on his own. Yesterday, I heard, was very hot. Did you swim for the first time? Does your son bring you absolute joy? I fell ill with a stomach ache and have barely been able to recover from it.

Not a day has gone by these past six weeks that a mention of his *Conquest of Peru* or a rendering of his noble face has not appeared in an article, written up with importance in the daily papers. In the early weeks you tried to avoid it, but it couldn't be managed for long. Earlier in the day you pulled the newspaper out of your pocket, sat and unrolled it on the uneven floor, and began examining it several times through while the sun made you sweat down your back. The writer continued in long passages about how Prescott arose in the early hours of the morning, not even saying hello to his wife or children, but sitting and writing straight though before taking lunch at one o'clock, then returning to his study alone. In the evenings he would craft his book reviews and on the weekends would partake in the "literary loafing" he had been saving up as a reward for a hard week's work. That Prescott should have — at the age of twenty-five, ailing not merely from his eye's suffering but from the rheumatism that affected his limbs — aspired wholly to the character of literary historian and hero, when all the documents were then composed in a language entirely alien to him, and when the sources and accounts conflicted so variously and described a time and place so far removed from his own, with no help from anyone or anything but his own natural genius, totals an effort of such magnitude I think it has never before been set upon by anyone prior to my friend. In the beginning, to redouble his efforts, and with his natural, simple-hearted, and buoyant manner, he took to making bets, as he had with Mr. Bentham who supposed he was owed — or owed — in the region of two thousand dollars over a manuscript Prescott was said to be working on, and every few months Prescott would go into his office and, laughing, hand him twenty dollars or ask for thirty or twenty in return, which Mr. Bentham would produce, never growing too out of pocket because of it. Or Prescott would enter with a sheet for him to sign, the sheet folded over so he could not see the terms. But knowing it was all in good humour and designed to spur Prescott to activity, he did not see the harm in doing it. It was because Prescott felt a life of dainty, elegant idleness was freely open to him — and with his buoyant, simple-hearted nature, was as likely as any young man of his time to take that path — that he had to devise such complicated means to get himself to work. For work, at seven hours a day, in its endurance and because of his God-given talents, was the only way to achieve any measure of happiness in this world, though he disliked work and was, he claimed, by nature idle. It was a principle of industry that led him to write his great books of history, though

because of his infirmity he could as easily have neglect-
ed it. But earnest industry it was, and some subject to
which he could devote serious and constructive labour
was essential if not to leave the graver periods of man-
hood without its appropriate interests, and old age
without its proper respect. But this was something that
had not occurred to him until his twenty-eighth year,
before which time he was dainty and elegant in the
manner of all the men he knew, and dined out and
drank every night of the week without any thought to
his health, or to the happiness of his wife, or to his life's
own labours, though the men he met with regularly
were already being taken to work in the banks and the
law offices of their fathers. But in time his life demanded a different foundation from all this, one deeper and
more solid and which could only be found in the application of his mind to a subject that could consume his
lively interest. *Be occupied always*, he instructed himself
more than once around this time, and later notes he
wrote to himself continue the refrain: *These past three
months have slipped by and I don't have anything to show for
it. I have worked lazily enough or have been too lazy to work
at all. Fortunately for the good economy and progress of the
species, activity — mental or physical — is indispensable to
happiness.* And again, *I find it hard to get anything under
way. I can't stand the repetition of work. The sum total of
what I have done in this dizzy winter has left me in my
worst health and worse spirits than in all winters previous,*

and I am wasting my talents in the great Taskmaster's eye.
Though he went away from his work whenever it gave
him pause — out for visits to the countryside, away
from his desk to sit with Claire — he had the resolve to
return to what he was doing without too much delay,
and in order to incite himself to work, considered insti-
tuting a series of fines for lapses which he would give to
charity. But he too much liked giving to charity and had
too great an income from his father's wealth for it to
help much. It was public humiliation he feared more,
and so, as it was with Bentham, he would make bonds
or agreements with his college friends, payment subject
to failing to write two hundred and fifty pages by this
time next year or something else, the object being, as
he said, *to prevent further vacillation until I have written*
so much of it as to secure my interest in going through with
it, as perhaps the desire to work does not always
come to actually working. In time and with practice, he
would be sitting all through the mornings, then straight
through the evenings after dinner and writing through
the night, and only when giving himself consciously to
relaxation would he take pleasure in his wife and whatever charms he found in her. It was several years after
his marriage — twenty months had passed since the idea
first came to him until the actual laying down of words
on paper — when he found all his careful planning had
been mistaken as the work grew and grew beneath his
hands. He had intended from the start to make one

modest volume of it, but it was not long before he gave up the struggle to keep it down to two. Similar troubles he encountered all the way along, and what influenced the whole of his subsequent life was his technique, developed in those months, of letting events tend to some obvious point or moral. In short, paying attention to the development of events as one would to the construction of a romance or drama, and in this way lending an *interest* to history as well as a utility. A further ten months brought him to the end of the third chapter, another month to the end of the fifth. My friend, at this point in his early marriage, was going at such a rate as to make his history fill ten volumes, and the whole world is not sorry that at last he settled on three. Such troubles encumbered him all the way through his work — the erection of new plans, the collapse of old ones. Though the space he filled overran his estimate, he was not alarmed and felt he was making progress and took courage. At half past ten, having poured himself a final glass of wine, he would retire to bed and fall quickly asleep, and sleep soundly and well. He gave up early suppers, though they were a form of social intercourse much enjoyed in his father's house and continued to be common in the circle to which he belonged, but alongside all other factors against him was that, in time, and after a day of working from the earliest until he could work no more, he found that the lights commonly placed on the table shot their horizontal rays so as to injure his eye. Larger evening parties were not so liable to produce this offence and he preferred them for the pleasure they gave rather than any social influence they might confer. If a violent storm prevented him from going out, or if the bright snow on sunny days in winter rendered it dangerous for him to expose his suffering organ to its brilliant reflection, he was nevertheless faithful and exact, as he was in all things, and would dress himself for the street and walk vigorously about the colder parts of the house, or would chop firewood, wrapped in a blanket, being, in the latter case, read to all the while. The first mile or two of his daily walk often caused him pain, but he never on this account gave it up, for regular exercise in the open air was, he knew, indispensable to the preservation of whatever remained of his decaying sight. Earlier in life, when enjoyment came more easily and he could stay out later, he would, on the coldest winter nights, after returning home and in order that his system be refreshed and his sight invigorated for the next morning's work, run tirelessly up and down a plank walk that had been arranged in the garden of his Beacon Street house so that he was able to do it with his eyes shut, for seventy minutes or more.

WHEN I HAD GONE that morning in a friendly way to receive his opinions and advice and he suggested I see the Bro_n, I could not think of how to respond. I was surprised my friend would treat me like that. The whole thing had become clear from general conversation that the only benefit of the exhibit was that it could occupy the man who does not value his time. Would he advise Amory to take his wife to this show? Just because I do not receive the papers daily does not mean I should be tricked into thinking the critics have been hailing Bro_n, who will always be an apprentice. I am, along with all reasonable men, a great lover of sincerity in art, and in order to have sincerity we must have detail, and the whole world is aware by now that J_nfon produces the most detailed faces and the most modelled hands. He is an absolutely conscientious artist, while an epidemic of crazy laughter prevails before the Bro_n. I read it myself: *Is the painter motivated by real conviction? If so, he is to be respected and pitied. But as with all false convictions, one could prove that the results are also false. If he had even a little passion he would surely arouse* someone, *because there are still twenty of us in this country who have a taste for novelty, yet obviously he belongs to a school which, failing to recognize beauty and unable to feel it, has made a new deal of triviality and platitude. He ought to steer closer to the well-won lessons of the masters, whom he seems to desire to imitate.* I will not see the Bro_n and I will not purchase a catalogue. I despise the galleries anyway. Nothing so exquisitely refined should live in such cramped quarters, like a dog in a cage. *Quand le bâtiment va, tout va!* With my eyes in the state that they are in, it cannot be risked. Perhaps I will say, *This* is why you suggested I see the Bro_n, when everyone is talking about the J_nfon. You wish to damage my optic nerve! Whether the topic is "modern art" or "modern life," he never fails to trick me into adopting the inferior attitude.

Everything has always been for him without effort at all. *Now I propose to break ground on my* Mexico, he wrote on the third of February. *I shall work the mine, however, at my leisure. Why should I hurry?* And hurry he did not, but rather put it off so that three months were passed in loafing before he was able to sit down at his desk, beginning only a few days labour for it was to be another six months before he would again put a word on paper, given the interruption of a voyage to Nigeria on account of his daughter's ill health and the death of his brother Edward at sea, two things which together prevented him from coming to his labours for another half year. After an autumn and winter passed in this way, he found himself occupied with so many social engagements that, in total, with these interruptions and the gaiety of town life and his buoyant nature which forbade him from ever passing up an opportunity to dine with friends, it was altogether eleven months before he sat down to his papers and discovered the whole plan mistaken, having thought it would take him one year to write one hundred pages, when he ended up spending a year and a half on one hundred and twenty. Though having chosen his topic, he hesitated; at last, after reading Alfieri's life to quicken his courage, he began to work in earnest. *I find it very difficult*, he wrote, *to screw up my wits to the historic pitch; so much for the vagabond life I have been leading, and breaking ground on a new subject is always a dreary business*. After putting down the first sentence on the fifth of August, he continued for several days, writing one and a half pages each day, not pausing to consider whether his plan was a good one or not, but picking up his pen would not stop or step from his desk until one and a half pages had been written, and if he reached such a pitch that would have allowed him to write more, he would always stop in order to reserve his energies for the next day's work. Around that time, working swiftly and in such a way and with no thought to the future, he wrote Mr. Gardiner that his happiness had never been so much assured *as it has been this past month, when work on the book is so steady, and so regular, and makes the whole of my life feel sure.* He was less troubled by his eye and had not yet reached the state of his infirmity when composing entire chapters in his head became necessary and his whole approach required new efforts. Although at times the weather caused him additional impairment, he remarked that there was no difference in his work on these days, and realizing this, he took courage and worked well. Even when he was not feeling well he worked harder than any man I have ever known, yet never in a prideful or boastful manner, for all the inspiration he needed was his material — so well chosen to perfectly match his interests — and his regular habits of industry, which, once he settled upon, he never wavered from, never questioned, and would not complain about. Sitting and thinking till day broke, he would await his young assistant who would enter by ten and begin transcribing, or, on alternate days, would pick up reading from where they had left off in the nine thousand pages of research Prescott had amassed. Having the good gift of being able to keep so much of it in his mind, Prescott would dictate clearly and well, never trifling with style but the style flowing naturally from his lips. In this way, it was not a year and a half before he had completed the first draft of his *Conquest of Mexico*, while in the same time, no man who had earned the respect of the literary journals had completed even a quarter of any work that was to prove more important or more finely crafted than this fine volume which he spoke of only rarely, only when pressed, and even then in general terms, never appearing troubled by it, and never admitting to any difficulties. As he said, *A writing man should never admit his doubts*, thinking it would only increase them and hamper his productivity. His letters to the Boston Law Library show a record of his days: *Industry good and with increased interest. Spirits — an amiable word for temper — improved.* And, on the day following, *Best recipe: occupation with things, not self.*

Now the sound of thunder comes into the city and the rain is pouring down, rushing through the gutters, and drenching the trees and me and everything. On my left there are rosebushes, and on my right, a huge expanse of lawn. I cannot go to the Prescotts' smelling like a wet dog, my suit all wet and my feet all wet, ruining the chairs and dripping down. He has not returned to me the article, the one I have been labouring on for so long. It is only that I have laboured ten long years on this article that cannot be called great, and he has not returned it or acknowledged my letters. Even walking past his house on days I thought he would be outside, he was not; the windows were shuttered and the door was locked. There had been a gardener working on his lawn in the summertime, watching me closely as I passed. I continued by him and went down the block and around the next; but when autumn arrived even the gardener was gone. At first I hoped something had befallen him, or that he had shut himself off and retreated into the seclusion of his home. But soon I discovered that he and Claire were entertaining as usual, and that he was healthy and not the least bit disturbed. It wasn't until later that I learned that his parlour had been filled with representatives from every state and territory in the Union: a lawyer from the General Court of Massachusetts, a friend of Governor Andrews and an acquaintance of one who had swum the Tiber, keepers of the mansions on Tory Row, another whose daughters were said to be like figures out of the Vita Nuova, all of them taking meals at the Supper Club, the Five of Clubs, the Adirondack Club, and the Malthusian League. There were celebrants from Lowell's fortieth birthday, the editor of the *North American Review*, practitioners of the vasectomy and the salpingectomy, utilizers of Darwin's doctrine of evolution, and, with the possible exception of Matthew Arnold, the ablest critical essayist of our time; also friends of Mr. Ward in Washington, the son of Cabot and the son of Holmes, abstainers, dog breeders, writers of verse in wartime, Curtis, Palfrey, Hoar, and Shaw, and one whose ancestors were said to be Puritans in every line of descent from as far back as the time when Puritanism was first known, the grandson of the widow of the Sheriff of Gloucestershire, Montague Crackanthorpe, collectors of funds for the Museum of Natural History, and lecturers from every capital in the region.

My invitation to the Prescotts' might as well have fluttered into my hands from a branch in a tree, having been swept out of the pocket of Benjamin Pierce on his morning constitutional.

I am shortening my life with this obstinacy and immoderation, having for too long admired their flowerbed, though it's now just a puddle from the earlier rain. This wavering you call Prescott. But Prescott's inside. Either you will eat tonight or you won't, and whether Prescott will notice, you can be sure Claire will be concerned until she discovers in the morning whether you were all right. Yes and no. You will plead off her help and sympathy and she will invite you again. The evening is wasted anyhow, by now. The district restaurants have closed and you will have to leave the pie on the lid of a garbage can for some cats. Though the pie is ruined, the night is not yet completely ruined, and it's possible that once inside you will be swept up in the bright lights and the excitement and Prescott engaging you and the questions you can answer better than most. No, not better than most. Than some. The questions you can answer, if only one or two. Then I will eat and drink and laugh a bit, and pull on my coat and return to my home without a partner accompanying me up the stairs to my room, and without even the promise of a woman. Unless I turn out to be exceedingly charming, which I can be and have been at these suppers before. If tonight Claire has invited a hopeful sister whom she has told about me, about what kind of a man I really am, honest and trustworthy and fair, an old friend of William's. She can vouch for my character. I have a pie. It's a little ruined, I laugh, but come — and we hurry into the kitchen together, bumping legs in front of the stove, laughing as she pours me a glass of wine, then back to the large and warm dining room with several people, ten, seven, seventeen, sitting all around it, but two seats reserved for us, me putting my drink at my plate, beside hers, and I return mugging to the kitchen once more with Claire, her shooing me out, then back to the table with Prescott's announcement and how he read the article I published — a toast. Everyone agrees, and a toast! The woman's eyes are glowing beside me as I shrug modestly and let it go, shrug it off with one quick line and a wink, then take half the glass in one gulp robustly, then the roast, then the potatoes passed around — and the sister beside me is bumping her arm into mine, she's left-handed, embarrassed about that, and I show her I too can eat with my left hand and she laughs, the tears disappearing from her eyes. No, I'm safe as her sister said, a good man and genial too. No reason to be scared, if not a little scared. I am after all a bachelor who lives alone, and what could my articles be about? Claire opening the door to me and the sister standing behind her, eyes lighting up. Or Prescott and no sister until I walk through the parlour and she's on a chair, not looking up but blushing, and Prescott with his pipe in his mouth is taking me by the arm and whispering into my head the rosy sister's name. Or just Prescott opening the door and a blank look from him before a little smile, polite, and the slow and dreary walk to the dining room, already the plain-faced friends of Prescott at the table, watching me arrive. Oh, another. The pie ruined and apologies for it. Claire at the table, taking the pie with a little smile of thanks, though disappointed, and a look to Prescott, *Here's your friend, late again*. They have been keeping dinner warm but Prescott only nods as we sit down, and still I'm making apologies while everyone wants to talk about something else and no one mentions the article because what article could they mention? There is no article, but maybe if I. I could have written it tonight if Prescott had not invited me for supper, knowing he didn't want me there really and that I'd almost not show, as usual ringing the bell too late, his oldest friend. But I didn't know the meal had begun! If only I had started out on time. If I had just begun my journey when I first put on my coat and not let myself put down the letter first. Had I left the house one minute earlier I would have caught the streetcar, or if the pie had been ready sooner. The neighbours arranged for a party last night, so I had to sleep with the earplugs in and woke up with a headache. You know how dusty it is in my apartment. You think I'm terrible, but I tried my best. I'm sorry. So sorry. So sorry I am late. Please forgive me. Oh, but wasn't it to start at ten? I thought you said ten! I thought you said ten. Put the pie in the flowerbed. Leave now. There is a standing here and a standing here and nothing more. You have given ten of the best years of your life over to this sort of work, and it has been entirely imperfect industry.

There has always been one way to go about finding out what sort of a man you are, and that is to go straight to people and return to yourself. You walk alone on a clear night, that is all. Why doubt your honesty? What is resting its eyes on you in a disquieting way? Here you are now — the gleaming snow, the smooth road, frost, silence — and still you lack the courage to think what you're thinking. I do not lack the courage to think. Nothing will convince me that everything he does is not meant to elevate himself in the esteem of other men. Yet he is the one you love, and not the gentler Amory. But you do not love him as you profess to, to him and to yourself. You love him in a cold way. It wasn't always in my mind this way, but he has changed somewhat. After the success of his book there was a slight change of emphasis. I would have liked to sit closer, but other people pushed in beside him and he didn't seem to care. Even tonight it will be no different. If you had wanted, you could have stayed in and never heard any protest from anyone. It is only because I preserve his letters that he keeps on inviting me. This is fine. You are completely incapable of flattery! Whereas once you saw everyone's merits, now you see only their faults. His life is clearer and more agreeable than most. Better for you to turn around, absolutely. There is less reason for you to be here than you suppose. This kind of crisis is not worth an ant colony, not even an ant. Go back to bed. Cover your feet. You are worn out and very bitter and have yet begged no one to help.

There were no books when I was a boy. Had I seen a book I would have thought it was a foreign object. I would have made it do tricks. I would have given it a bowl of food and waited for it to eat. There were other boys who were more sophisticated than I, who grew up to do great things, and there is no experience in their lives equivalent to the one I had with books. Yet they would not be able to see this as I do. This is the reason — I do blame it — for my status today, and that while other people have been able to move ahead in the world, I have found myself, for the past ten years if not more, standing with the very same sights before me, a fact that has not been overlooked by friends who have come to visit and to whose houses I have gone. They have commented, freely, on the state I find myself in, thinking I could have had a different life if only I'd lived it differently. You'll have to get used to it. Thank God there are so many of them. A man who has made something of himself can only believe he gained success from an application of will; that had he been in my place, these ridiculous events could have been avoided. How can I expect to achieve what I love in life? There is a certain smell that pervades my clothes and it is this that prevents opportunities from coming to me. It is just that these agonizing memories evoke the need to talk about them. I mean that this smell is not disconnected to the lack of books in my childhood. You cannot believe that. I think there is something that — call it a smell if you will — emanates from my body and betrays what kind of man I am today and the position I have secured for myself, which, despite great effort, is slight. I was invited to dine with Mr. William H. Prescott tonight. He is a childhood friend. These people I am growing old with are living exactly the same lives as when they were young. It doesn't matter. What matters is that the smell I am speaking of causes it to go no further than the ache of company. It is something they pick up on. I use very good soap. Pears. It is raining and thawing. I trace it back to when I was a boy and it is my absolute right to do so! In my field of aspiration, it is like having been born without a foot. But I never complain and few people know I feel that way.

I am adding this: There was a neighbour I loved as a child and his wife died. I did not see him for six or seven months following that, but when we did finally meet we talked only about the article I had long been working on. We did not talk about his wife at all.

There was a woman who approached me once. She was small and she smiled, standing there in the street, so I accepted from her hand the marriage pamphlet, which went on to praise the institution for not only preventing disease, but for focussing the minds of men like myself, who would otherwise be more likely to dissipate their energies. My question was: How can the natural instincts reasonably be gratified without infringing upon the rights and happiness of others? Good women are rare, and for a man of a certain type to find himself with one — often it is exactly these women who will raise a man out of the squalor in which he is living. The man who does not seize on an opportunity to be saved will seldom be saved. Her hands looked so soft, but she could not speak — or would not — and after handing the pamphlet to me, ran off to rejoin the army of girls who were rushing up and down the road, in and out of the rooming houses.

Around the time of his marriage, my friend was one of the finest looking men I ever saw. He had been labouring eight long years on his first great work, and fitted the house on Beacon Street to his wants and infirmities, then carefully added luxuries: a present from his grandmother and grandfather, but no less a part of his nature. It's the gilt-lined walls, the chandeliers, the silkwood cabinets, the rugs and china pots and framed mirrors, the hand-carved arches between the rooms, and everything else to which I can't give a name.

My speckled lamp is very nice, though nicer when it isn't on. Still, everyone who visits remarks. No reason to think of moving. Wherever you'd end up would be full of dust in the same way, the same thick air and smell of smoke and the kitchen always without bread. It's good to stay in exactly the same place, where at least if some friend should visit, perhaps from out of town, they'd know where to find you without having to ask.

Tomorrow I will have to start the work on my room that I have been putting off. You put it off and put it off, but in case someone should come by you might sweep up a bit, take the papers off the floor and put them on your desk. Put the papers on your desk and sweep up the floor. Dust off the lamps. Pay the three bills that are resting on the umbrella stand and throw out the newspapers. Send them off tomorrow. Reply to Putin. Put away the plate near the bed and hang out the sheets. Allow five months for it.

THE BATH WATER WAS COLD when I pulled myself from the tub, dripping down. I looked about me for a towel, but all of the towels were gone. They were not hanging in the bathroom or lying on the floor. They were in the other room, which was filled up with smoke. I would have to go and dry myself in there, and the bath — a waste; the smoke sticking to my skin, stinking me up again. Exhausted and near tears, I went to the mirror. I often go to the mirror when crying, to see how I might look. I wonder whether I'd have any sympathy for a man such as myself. Sometimes I feel I would, and it makes me cry even harder; other times I do not and it fills me with despair — well, then I weep more pitifully than before. In these ways I find I am able to enjoy myself. The pure times I spend alone are rare.

All my life I have been on the lookout for the consolation in things. So long as one's sensitiveness is to run from the rough impact of life, it is neither strenuousness nor austerity that one needs, but only consolation.

When Mary went away it was years before we heard from her, though even in that letter she did not say much. *I trust you are engaged on some high historical subject*, she wrote only to Prescott, and he did not respond. *I wish you could see the pretty pictures under my window*, she wrote in the letter following that one, and in the final note, *Do say if you can come and stay some time — I must not close without saying how much I think of you, now that the Thames is covered with swans.* Prescott told me this in an offhand way, left the letters out for show, which I didn't want to see but pulled at anyway to read straight through, beginning to end. He gathered them up, laughing, put them in his drawer and latched it up with a slender key, then slipped it into the pocket of his pants, securing it there with an extra pat. Claire was in the next room preparing the tea, while Prescott sat far back in his chair and smiled in a way I was not meant to understand. I could not speak at all. There she was, shut up in his drawer, and he licked his lower lip, grinning to the gums, a disgusting habit he acquired when he was seventeen. Then inquiring whether I had heard the latest by way of Amory, the tale descended into a filth I could not hear in relation to Mary without shaking. Of course, he said, he had thought of sending her money, but then Claire would know, and as Claire kept all the books there couldn't be any way. We would just have to accept it. *You are now, I believe, working on a project far more brilliant than any of your fellow countrymen. You must think, by the length of my yarn, that I really believe you to have returned to private life and have nothing in the world to do.* He pushed the key against his thigh so I could see it hidden there.

It had been so long since I'd received a nice letter, and when I finally did, I did not reply to it at once, though I thought of her often. In time, on the twenty-fifth of June, I finished it quickly and sent it off. The whole affair had been on my mind for seven and a half weeks. When a person needs justification, time will elapse. What a person wants is a lapse in bed and time for self-pity. Convalescence. What do you do when someone important remembers your name in a flowery setting? I was too young then to have taken it seriously. I was a contributing editor. That's where I know your face from, she had said. Oh. It had never happened before, and I wondered whether she was thinking of another. Women don't care for my company, except one or two. Yet I was privileged to have enjoyed what little of it I did. But what did you make of it, then? You were unable to show her off, to impose on everyone the burden of such a woman, to force others to spend time in her difficult presence. There was nothing about her that could show them the qualities you wished you possessed: whatever is impeccable with no fault at all. But that was not the sort of woman you loved, when you did. I did try to find a woman like Claire for myself, but there was no woman I ever met as devoted, and, at the time, as beautiful. Even if you had found a good woman, you would not have had as fine a life as Prescott, to whom everything comes so naturally, and before whom the whole world opens itself up, bestowing upon him all of God's gifts. After he married Claire there could be no hope of things going back to the way they were before, and after that it was only she who determined the flow of their lives. He could not, any more than completely stop breathing, go through a single day without her, and this feeling never wavered, as Prescott wrote to me in a letter, *Contrary to the assertion of La Bruyère — who somewhere says that the most fortunate husband finds reason to regret his condition at least once in twenty-four hours — I may truly say that I have found no such day in the quarter of a century that Providence has spared us to each other.*

If I were asked to name the man I have known whose coming was most sure to be hailed a pleasant event by all, I should not only place Prescott at the head of the list, but I could not place another man near him. The same as has been said about Prescott could be said of his dear friend Mr. Gardiner, whose pleasure in all social circumstances always lent a brilliance to every night, his arrival as much anticipated by men as by their wives. I have never known anyone whose company was as universally attractive as Mr. Gardiner's, equally to the young and the old and to all the classes that he mingled with, and never once did I hear him disparaged, being, as he was, unfailingly polite and attentive, never forgetting anyone's name and always shaking my hand with eagerness. Never were there two men who, by natural constitution, shared a keener zest for social involvement, displayed a greater ease in all circumstances, went into them more willingly, and could drink and smoke in such moderation yet still enjoy the evening to excess. On Prescott's face was commonly the expression many men wear of that rapture in love that is so contagious, a smile as natural to him as the feeling of hunger in others, and I think no man ever walked our streets who attracted such esteem or infected others more with his giddy laughter, which at times would overtake him to such a degree that, in a woman, we would think such convulsions hysteria. Whatever ludicrous idea it was that affected him he seldom succeeded in communicating, yet the infection of laughter would spread from one to another until a whole party would be perfectly ruined with it, none of whom could have told what in the world he was laughing at unless it were the sight of Prescott, so utterly overcome and struggling in vain to express himself. It was that Prescott experienced greater varieties of happiness than any man previously born, and could enjoy more — and more easily — than any of those with whom I've been acquainted. His capacity for both giving and receiving the highest degree of pleasure in social entertainment found its happy match in Mr. Gardiner, and it is their capacity for pleasure that has long made their attendance so desired by any hostess, whose invitations might be half-written before realizing she forgot to question Prescott about other engagements that night or inquire whether Mr. Gardiner might be available, then tearing up all her note cards and beginning over again.

It was dark and the whole day was darkening and was dark already when I awoke on the floor, feeling miserable. There was no time for a shave, no time to do anything, so I found my belt and put it around my waist and discovered the matches in the bottom of a drawer and my cigarettes in the stove. It was calm and quiet and the room was dim, and as I looked through the glass I felt myself to be truly in an old baronial fortress, my face drawn tight. I put the cigarettes in one pocket and the matches in the other, then I flipped them, the cigarettes now more comfortably in the right pocket and the matches in the left, so that when I walked about the room, testing, they both felt more secure. One of my pockets is smaller than the other and I'd rather lose my matches than all my cigarettes. Then it occurred to me that it might be best to leave them at home and bring only one or two and not by accident overdo it, showing up at the Prescotts' smelling of smoke, not fit for dinner, and dragging the street in with me. It is fine for a rich man to smell of tobacco since often it is a nice brand, and because he's well off you don't suspect his health, while a man in a suit too small can't help but arouse the fear of germs one hasn't even considered. But it was growing too late to be thinking such things, so I hastily put two cigarettes in the one pocket and the matches in the other. I had to leave at once if I wanted to fulfil the requirement, a nine o'clock arrival, while it was already a quarter past, so I quickly moved the cigarettes to the other pocket and put the matches in the opposite, and stepping about a little to see how it felt, it seemed to me as though the cigarettes would fall out on their own. It's true I shouldn't smoke them at all. It is one thing for a rich man to smell of tobacco, arriving at a party with fine cigarettes laid out neatly in a case, but it is quite another for a man such as myself to arrive at a party smelling of smoke, a bunch of cigarettes making more lumpy his already lumpy coat, or to bring along one or two as though he could only afford to buy them in pairs.

The cigarettes were now completely out of the question. I was not so weak I could not go one evening without them. In any case, night had been coming on and was now long on and I would have to hurry if I wanted to arrive no later than the nine-thirty arrival for all. I went to the door, then returned for the key and at once grew concerned about my hair, that the oil I had used made it look gaudy. But there could be no question of remaining home a moment longer. I was as dressed and ready as I could possibly be, so I put the cigarettes in my left pocket and the matches in the right, then hurried them to the opposite pocket, then left.

Now YOU GO AND SEE the Maslovs with a bunch of faded mauve and yellow flowers in hand. If I know I will not be attending I try to contact the host, but sometimes I'm too weak to do even that. Naturally I dislike most forms of communication and often there isn't time. If ten years pass and I find myself without friends, this failing will be the cause. I don't pretend that things are all right the way I have them. My manner of life is, like everyone's, patchwork. This is the reason — if anyone had the interest to look into it — why I've ended up the way I have. But I do not frequently tell people this. I don't expect them to care. I don't expect my gift will pass for greatness since my taste is not so good. I am aware that they are faded. You could still exchange them. But all the flower exchanges are closed. I am going to blame the rain. Naturally I long to brighten my flowers with some red or pink ones, even some greenery. If you were to abandon it now there wouldn't be a second failure, which you can see, and not far off.

At this point there is no other way it could occur. There are two ways it could be, and if the one fails, it will merely involve more of a walk. An interpretation: looking for red flowers — the search for new joys; looking for leaves — the search for hope. If you wanted to have dinner you should have gone to the Prescotts'. Yes, but the Maslovs haven't started so I won't be as late. Besides, I like the disorder in the way they attend to it. I like that the silverware and china are spotted. That sort of thing relaxes me. They say only God can judge a husband and a wife, and I don't object. I don't pretend to understand what they do for so many hours of the day. I can imagine Prescott taking walks and dictating, and Claire doing whatever she must to maintain the house. Everything is spoiled now, but it was different when we were children. Today I can't get anyone who knows him to agree with any of my criticisms. At the time, this wasn't a problem. Now pretty much nobody can be brought to see it from my side of things. I don't expect it. When he has made a mistake, all he can do is move forward. Probably they will not invite me again. Is it my fault I prefer the Maslovs? You can't control these things. What a storm. He doesn't say it, but no doubt he has others he prefers above me. Amory. All those who have published books. I deliberately put on my favourite suit and I will not show up so nicely dressed just to be mocked to my face! I have only published a smattering of articles and I am well aware he finds me tedious because of it. This includes being matched up with one of Claire's hideous sisters, especially in front of all those people, as though I have troubles in this area well known enough for them not to be subtle in the way they go about it. I didn't put myself through a rigorous wash at seven tonight only to be made a fool of, as I know would have happened if I had gone. The fact of my being his oldest friend only makes it worse than if he had chosen me in the midst of his success. My presence seems to everyone an obligation, like inviting a brother. All this *particularly* after tidying myself and putting careful thought into how I would look. Wilcox is the only one who has any sense of humour at all — not only about herself but about his work — and that is the reason she isn't invited any more. Since he stopped inviting her, the evenings have become dull. No, I don't want any part of it if Wilcox is not invited. I will tell them precisely this the next time they invite me. If they won't ask Wilcox they shouldn't ask me! I might visit her instead. Though we would have nothing to say, particularly not in private. But at least we wouldn't have to talk about her book. Of course, I don't have an invitation. In the end, she's not my physical type and is a little too crude. Besides, she's young and somewhat frivolous. If he really wishes to see me, he can call and meet me separately. I have no time for it. I have my own work to do, even if he doesn't believe it. You might find a streetcar. But not one has passed. I haven't seen a single streetcar the entire night. Just keep going in that direction. You don't have much to say, but they are always happy to see you, and not because of some arbitrary connection passed down from your grandfathers. Oh, what a bore. There's no use trying to correct it now. Wandering around like some drunk, some fool. Awnings! They don't protect, just funnel more of the rain onto you! It has already proved to be a failure, and nothing could redeem it. Right now they are enjoying each other, each one of them, telling stories and laughing in the warm light of the Prescotts', and so happy and easy and warm around the table at the Maslovs'. Look around. Having no wife obviously accomplishes all this. See how free I am? I'm carrying out the directions with an ingenuity and fidelity all my own. At least if there must be a criticism it will come not from a friend or from the critics. Put them down. They're completely wilted. I thought they were nice when the evening began. Well, you were wrong. You can't accuse the rain. Had you thought it over even once or checked outside before you left, you would have known to bring an umbrella. There, hair all wet, suit all wet, just sitting down you would have completely ruined the chairs. Appearing on their doorstep like a wet dog. There is no guessing how much shame you would have caused. Oh, what of it. So it rained. It is not my fault it rained.

The passage home had been dispiriting, meant to last ten days, but it was twenty-two I spent on that boat in a long, ugly dream of longing. When I arrived home, there on the deck in the afternoon sun — coming or going, I could not tell — was Amory dressed in a dark suit with an umbrella tucked under his arm. So pleased was I to see a familiar face for the first time in so many months that a smile came over me and I waved. He looked at me, then looked away as I continued to smile broadly, then hid my teeth behind my lips, my lips behind my hand, and began to weep for the first time since news of my father's death had come to me, forcing me to leave London for home.

A porter retrieved the trunks and I followed behind him as he led me down the dock. On the voyage back I had passed long hours on the ship in silent daydreaming, in the little room with the bunk that was mine. It had been a fortuitous letter from Prescott that determined I would return home at once. It indicated the formation of a club whose members he proudly listed, the purpose being the discussion of all things literary, and the idea of producing a little journal for recording for posterity the scribblings of its members had even been proposed. There were Bliss, Blazer, Dawson, Atkins, Charles Folsom, Dexter, Addison, and others. Prescott would be the editor. I had grown so eager to see my friend, whose note had aroused in me such a fine picture of this manner of moral acquaintanceship — but the life that awaited me when I returned was one from which all light had been excluded. Perhaps I should not have gone and then returned in that easy way. Perhaps you never should have left at all. For months I anticipated the invitations that would greet me. Nothing came. A note of condolence from my father's creditor, and from the rest, a silence so total I felt I was living in a room without sun.

When Mary came to my door, I let her in. I listened as she sat on the edge of the sofa in our little parlour and listed off all she had worked out, beginning to end, about her voyage to Europe and what she hoped to find. You sat without speaking as she told you all her plans. If a privileged woman wanted to fill her life with misery, she could have it. Then I heard my mother calling and told her I had to go. If a man is to spend a whole night with a woman who may be infected — of course it will not be so easy to apply disinfection successfully, as it would be if he merely had contact with the woman across the couch for a moment or two. If you leave a gun out in the mist for a few minutes, it is easier to clean than if you have left it out in the rain all night. It was my hope that she would not return or write me any more letters. I had not found my fortune in Europe and wished her luck would be as ill as mine. I walked her to the door and could tell that she wanted one last glance. I shut the door and went straight into the kitchen where I made my mother a soup, placing in it carrots, onions, and half a potato, to thicken up her blood.

AT HOME I'D SLEPT for several hours then awoke to a blue light and in a foul mood. Since the invitation, each day had been spent putting off thinking about it, and if anyone had approached with a suggestion about where to escape to, I would have gone without much thought. Instead, I traded in my suit for a new, nearly good one. I exchanged the laces in my shoes. I had long been occupying my mind with errands to distract myself from the coming fact of tonight, not wanting to imagine what would become of such a failure. But I was determined to go out into the streets, and if I failed I'd try again.

Prescott had written to tell me that his father had taken a fainting spell that morning at about eight o'clock, which terminated fatally. *Nathan who takes this will give you the account*, he had written. *We are all very tranquil, as my writing to you now shows. Do not come till after church, as nothing can now be done.* As a consequence, it was to be three whole months before he was able to return to his labours once again, and when he did, as he informed me in his clear-spoken voice, it was as if his mind had been wiped clean by a sponge, and the memory of his father and the loss that would always be with him was all that remained. He decided then to continue his work on the chapter following the one that had been broken off midway, and doing this he began solemnly and sat in his study with the letters of condolence that people had posted, pinned on one of the walls, the wall nearest his head. When I saw him the morning of the funeral he kept his head close to the gold-trimmed coffin, walking tight in behind it, so that when I asked about it later he replied only that it had been a windy day and the sand was up in the air, and that his father had one last time protected his eye from pain as he had done for him all his life, even up to the day of his death. He spoke of it in a calm and resolute way but was much preoccupied with the bond that had been so suddenly cut, the knowledge of which, he felt, would be with him always.

I arrived at once after I received the note informing me of the stroke his father had suffered, which ended fatally at eight in the morning, and arriving found the whole family sitting quietly on chairs in the living room, in each other's arms, crying quietly or sitting and staring at the wall or generally attending to the guests, of which there were many — young girls I had never seen before and friends of Prescott and Claire whom I did not know, who came bearing cakes on plates and casseroles and other dishes that they heaped on a counter in the kitchen. The deceased's own wife sat in the dining room, one of her sister's arms wrapped protectively around her, while I stood by and didn't know what was expected of me, and could not tell with certainty whether Prescott knew that I was there or not. It was not what I should have been thinking with his father so suddenly dead. How could I have expected him to be concerned with whether he was being polite to me, though he was not, or whether I was at ease and had anyone to stand with, which I did not. When Prescott did at last see me he came over and held me with a tenderness such as I had not felt since we were boys, and I was so moved and comforted by it. But that moment passed as suddenly as it began as Claire came up behind him and then moved in between us, and he let me go. I turned awkwardly and grasped her hand and gave her a small kiss on the cheek, perfumed and powdered and a little wet. Prescott told me to go to the kitchen and get myself some food, and he moved off with Claire to greet another friend, whose happy arrival disturbed and diminished mine, likely a man he had been awaiting far more eagerly — a gentleman and his wife and their two daughters in velvet, a well-known philanthrope with a taste for the arts. Turning from this scene, I made my way into the kitchen. I was not acquainted with the guests who gathered there, though one I was able to place from the papers and another was reminiscent of my boyhood at Pepperell. I did not speak with anyone but picked at the strands of coconut on a slice of cake I took, and failed to overhear any bit of gossip that might have been useful. They all kept their voices low and what I was able to discern concerned the feeding of horses.

Months later Prescott asked me, offhandedly, whether I had been at the house that day. Of course I had, I told him, and he apologized, smiling a little, explaining that he had been in such a state that, to this day, he could remember nothing of the weeks that followed his father's death except for flashes here and there, but nothing of the continuity of events or even whether he had slept or not, which I found hard to believe.

THE BLIND, FROM THE CHEERFUL *ways of men cut off, are cruelly excluded from the busy theatre of human action*, he wrote, and even signed his name to this article, too heated in its admiration of those we think of as deficient, but whose infirmity, he argued, was beneficial to men of learning, citing Democritus who had, as was related by Cicero, gouged out his own eyes that he might philosophize better, and Malebranche, who would shutter his room in the day if he wanted to think, preventing a single ray of light from entering; that without the distraction of worldly objects, the mind invariably turns inward toward contemplation, and how this, as well as the productive lives of the blind, give sufficient evidence of the worth of the human mind *and its capacity of drawing consolation from its own resources under so heavy a privation, so that it can not only exhibit resignation and cheerfulness, but energy to burst the fetters with which it is encumbered.* But everyone knows that it is better to be sighted than not, and that we look upon blindness as an infirmity is all that we need to prove it. Some lives are simply not worth living, and it is up to science, not morality, to discover whose. Yet Prescott dismissed this, and refused to speak to the danger of inviting the sick from all the corners of America into the centre of Boston. He insisted on the sincerity of his support for the Asylum, and that perhaps better men would be proud that in our city such a beneficent institution could be allowed to exist. But the experience of his own life from the time he was a boy had drawn him so far from the ordinary sympathies that he could not hold back from composing that broadside, so passionately and querulously worded, correcting in the proof sheets with as much severity. *Of one thing a writer may be sure*, Prescott had said, with the pride of a man who has received his diploma but has not yet had to use it. *If he adopts a manner foreign to his mind he will never please.* It was a circle of older men — Hughes, Sedgwick, Lyell, in whose trust Prescott's father had placed his well-being — who grew concerned, and agreed to see to it and so arranged it that the pamphlets, having been printed, remained folded in their boxes, all five hundred copies, to mould in the basement of the Asylum for the Blind. Time has of course elapsed, and everyone has since stopped thinking about it, but in the months that followed, it seemed to me that Prescott showed himself in society less and shut himself deeper into his house to work.

Seeking extra funds and with the intention of promoting as useful citizens the patients housed within, the Asylum for a time attempted to sell, in civic halls and churches, the fruits of those men and women who could not see their work: monstrous diapers and towelling, ill-stitched dress-shirts, straw and rush and thread and baskets that lacked even the charm of novelty. A selection of these frightful tokens was purchased on one occasion by a Catholic Father, but at a reduced price and not again. And while Prescott never again spoke against the eugenic law in the company of his high-minded friends, in the early days he would claim to have always found more danger in the powerful than the feeble, that he had never heard of a man who was weak terrorizing his family so much as one who was strong, and that the type of boy who likes teasing halfwits is not the sort to stand up to bullies. Yet he never criticized the movement among his friends or stated publicly his opinion of the feeble-minded bill — that it was a dangerous one, and that a law is like a dog: once released, it will follow its own nature, not yours.

WHEN MY FATHER DIED he left me nothing. My father loved me, but when he died, he gave me nothing. I remained standing at the cemetery gate, the lawyer at my back, reading out the will as I gazed into the hilly, stone-speckled field. I was left standing in the field, the lawyer close behind me like death on my shoulder, reading out the will in which my father gave me nothing. The lawyer had some things to say about it privately, after, as we sat together in a drinking-house. He was a man of my own age, slightly younger, and I asked to buy him a drink in a bar, close by, and we walked together through the grass which was soggy and had been dampened by that day's rain, and together went to a tavern on a corner in the little town where my father had been born.

In the earlier years, before Mr. Gardiner took a wife, he would dine with the Prescotts sometimes five times a week, his company enjoyed as much by Prescott as by

Claire. What secrets of chivalry Mr. Gardiner possessed it is impossible to say, but Claire never gave the
appearance of liking any of Prescott's other friends,
treating him almost as she would have her own son and
even arranging his marriage to a woman who had a little wealth of her own, some intelligence, and who was
young and so thoroughly admired Mr. Gardiner from
the start that a better match could not have been found.
You would so much have liked for them to find a kind
woman for you, a woman whose beauty and character
they admired, and to have them discuss it; that no other
man would be loved by her quite as well as you. Then
to sit with them in the parlour and for the four of us to
be so happy would have made such beautiful nights,
that Prescott would perhaps speak about them to others, and I would spend my days washing and dressing.
If I could have had that. But Claire never welcomed any
of Prescott's friends with the same natural warmth as
she did Mr. Gardiner, and always talked of Mr. Gardiner
without prompting. Even to your own mind Gardiner
is more worthy of respect. Did he ever say a word
against you, or refuse to shake your hand? Though he
was only a clerk, that did not prevent him from always
presenting to Claire the most beautiful of gifts — cut
glass bottles and coloured perfumes, little charms,
works of art, and all manner of things that never would
have occurred to you. If only you had taken sheets of
music, so finely notated, to which she could sing while

you played the piano, looking up and smiling. They always favoured Mr. Gardiner above me, but it wasn't till later that he proved his worth by editing each one of Prescott's fine volumes of history. He had spent three full weeks with the pages before meeting with Prescott and taking him through his notes, starting with the beginning and ending with the ending. Those nights spent looking over the manuscript often caused him to wake past noon, upsetting the order of his household. But that did not cause him to abandon his diligent industry, which led him to conclude that the trouble with the volumes lay in the feeling they gave to the reader that they would come to nothing. It was this that caused Mr. Gardiner to worry that the book would put off readers both at home and abroad, and it was at his suggestion of employing a rapidly building tension and dropping hints of the approaching tragedy that led Prescott to develop the style for which he is best known today, that of lending an *interest* to history as well as a utility. Having the story tend to some obvious point and moral came from that first, fateful consultation with Mr. Gardiner, after Gardiner had struggled three long weeks with the manuscript in his own home, reading it through twice before coming to the problem. After that, not two days passed without Gardiner's visiting their house, and while in the beginning he did not visit daily, as time went on he was there nearly every day, taking presents to Claire and spending the evenings after Claire had gone to bed, discussing the volumes with Prescott, and as time went on it came to be rumoured that Prescott could no longer write a single page without the help and guidance of his friend. It was Prescott alone who divined in Gardiner such a sensitivity, and though in time there were others who went to seek his help, it was Prescott who employed him first and best. Prior to that, he had worked as a law clerk, but so free and open was Mr. Gardiner with everyone he met that there wasn't a single man who could respond to him insincerely, and so, in this unlikely way, he quickly moved into the highest ranks and it wasn't long before he was a regular fixture at the dinners and in the homes of all those who travelled in Prescott's closest circle.

Mr. Gardiner suggested an important alteration in the arrangement of some of the early chapters, which served to bring out the theme and the thrust of the story. The history until that time had been a little slow in beginning, without giving any sense as to where the course of events was leading, or if it would continue as it began, giving no sign of change or catharsis, which, though it may be a history, a sincere story cannot do without, becoming all the more sincere because of it. It is not surprising that Claire looked well on Mr. Gardiner, as he offered so much to Prescott without asking anything in return. Mr. Gardiner accepted their loving hospitality with gratitude, as did all of those who were privileged to enjoy them, and never once did they put him out early or neglect to include him in whatever they were planning. Prescott was as certain of Mr. Gardiner's worth as he was of any of those with whom he enjoyed a fellowship, and after Mr. Gardiner suggested an important alteration in the arrangement of the early chapters, Prescott readily adopted it. On the day that Mr. Gardiner delivered the most fateful criticism of Prescott's career, he arrived without appointment at seven in the morning and proceeded to pace on the lawn outside the house until eight, at which point the gardener came out from behind the shed and let him into the house through the back. And so Mr. Gardiner went in through the kitchen, unusual for a guest, and encountered a startled Prescott, still in his pyjamas, drinking his morning tea. When Prescott excused himself to put on his day clothes, Mr. Gardiner stopped him and told him that he had to say right off what was in his mind, he had been up all night thinking — such loyalty is nearly impossible to come by — and so Prescott sat back down at the little breakfast table and Mr. Gardiner, not even accepting a cup of tea, began to lay it all out flat. The conversation lasted no more than twenty minutes, as Prescott has told it to journalists both here and across the Atlantic, and after those twenty minutes were through, Mr. Gardiner, blushing furiously now, took his leave and Prescott went straight away up to his study where he set upon the manuscripts, attacking them with a fresh burst of energy such as he had not felt since his twenty-ninth year, and allowed of no interruption that entire week, took no dinners socially, and wrote steadily and well, composing the histories over again so that they would come to some obvious point or moral, developing in that short week the style that has served to make him the success he is today. Prescott sat in silence during that twenty-minute conference, allowing himself not even a murmur of assent, and merely stood and shook hands with Mr. Gardiner at the end of it, Mr. Gardiner feeling within himself that Prescott's response was so plain because what he had just laid out was so true and right. As Mr. Gardiner tells it, he spent that day walking through Boston's parks, not returning home or alerting anyone to his whereabouts, but with a shiver spending the day alone in wonder at what he felt would change the world, knowing that the whole of Prescott's future would be forever altered, including his reputation, his life-long considerations about his own craft, and his daily method of work. *To influence a man*, as Mr. Gardiner has said in interviews in newspapers both here and abroad, *is the only proof a man has that he lives*.

II

IT CAME TO BE EXPECTED among all those who visited Prescott at his home in his later years that no one could pass the gentle, English "lady with the lamp" without her informing them that they were not to attempt to cheer the patient, nor to instruct him on remedies that an uncle of friend of a cousin had tried with much success, nor to question the rule of his doctors, nor to persist in saying, *I hope that it will please God to give you twenty years*, or, *You have a long life of activity before you*, as it was enough that he was suffering without having to assert to his friends the severity of his condition, or set right their hopes, or point out the likelihood of their prescribed remedies failing in his own case, the details of his condition being known only to very few — Claire, his doctors, and his nurse — the latter, a sound, close, keen observer, not merely sober and honest but a religious and devoted lady.

It was through the exertions of J. Fisher that there first came to be established the Asylum for the Blind, it being the earliest of such beneficent institutions that have proved their worth through their success both at home and abroad, and having become among the most advanced institutions in the world, it attracted the attention of Prescott. From nearly the very beginning he worked as a trustee and one of its most effective friends and supporters, beginning straight away and without delay his active service by writing a paper which positioned the Boston Asylum as a house working for the moral good, in a capacity not just scientific, but spiritual as well.

It was during the summer of his fifty-seventh year, when Prescott paused to have his eye examined while vacationing in England, that he made acquaintance with the nurse whom he was later to send for and establish in the Asylum, being himself of the belief that while nature alone cures, it is nursing's task to put the patient in the best possible condition for nature to act upon him. Not long after she was taken into service, many whose sight seemed to be weakening made progress, though for those who visited, the experience of being in the institution was a difficult one. Walking on tiptoe was discouraged, after her belief that doing anything in a slow manner in the room of one convalescing is particularly injurious; likewise she determined that there was to be no whispering outside the doors or inside the rooms, and there was to be no unnecessary noise for fear of inducing delirium. Starched petticoats and crinolines were no longer permitted, since such garments had the habit of upsetting the pots and candles and other implements, not infrequently igniting and burning their wearer to death. Then there was no end to the washing, by placing a steaming bowl beneath the limbs of those confined to their beds, and always the windows were to be pulled down at the top to allow ventilation and the doors closed to prevent draughts; also the fireplaces cleaned of soot and the walls scrubbed, bed sheets hung out once a day before the fire, and the pans emptied more than once every twenty-four hours — but only in the halls and never by the beds — and such a degree of all manner of changes that anyone who went to visit the home could see that the patients were very much improved. The reforms were instituted with difficulty at first, resisted by the nurses who had grown accustomed to their ways. But she felt, and made no secret of feeling, that in all the ranks and endeavours that require common sense and care, it is nowhere so little expressed as in nursing, which more often leaves those in need wanting, for the benefit of the indolence of those responsible for the care. It was only once the severity of Prescott's illness had become so great and Claire could no longer care for him and could not find a good enough substitute that they took the English woman into their home, her position at the Asylum left vacant for six chaotic months until a replacement was found. In the early days of her employment on Beacon Street, she would visit Prescott's room only at the appointed times, conducting all things with the quiet rigour and daily regimen she had devised while tending to the war-wounded, and her power over his health was like the magic of a sorcerer over birds. Yet in her intelligence was nothing supernatural, simply the minute observation of what affected him, and in all his time under her careful watch he never once found before him milk that was sour, meat that had turned, a bad egg or vegetables underdone, nor did he see or smell the food of others in the household, while all talk of food was forbidden, especially during the taking of it. No plate was left to linger by his side in case he should eat it, but was swiftly removed whenever he felt too unwell for even a spoonful of arrowroot in wine, much less an egg-flip.

When I went to visit Prescott while under her care, Claire was nowhere to be seen; there was only his nurse and two carefully attired ladies paying no special attention to anything but their own duties, and all his visitors were regarded as nuisances who more often left him ill at ease from their visits, given the stupidity of those who love the sick while not understanding them. We were made to understand that there was to be none of the shower-bath of silly hopes and encouragements so commonly heard by the ailing, and no more than ten minutes with the patient was permitted at one time, always supervised, and often terminating early at his nurse's discretion. It was soon determined among Prescott's friends that if there were some way of returning this woman to England, it would be far better.

Mr. Gardiner had made a present of his ginger harvest to Prescott the autumn before he was confined to his bed. I never gave them anything good, while Mr. Gardiner always knew what would please them most. He did not even have to ask what would please them, but had the happy habit of all treasured friends of always knowing exactly what would delight them best. He took the whole of his ginger harvest, which he'd had other men raise, and boxed it up in red and gold and made them a present of it, leaving it on their doorstep with no note, and only coming the next day to ask if they had any ginger to lend him, he who had no ginger. For the next two months, Claire took Prescott ginger cookies and duck in ginger sauce and steeped the ginger in their tea, and always Mr. Gardiner was with them to enjoy these treats. And there was not one night in the months following his generous gift that he did not dine with them both and then take Claire into his confidence after Prescott had been put to bed, worrying himself over Prescott's fate as his illness worsened. On the twenty-fourth of December, Prescott rose in his bedclothes and wrote from Boston to Lady Lyell, *A merry Christmas to you, dear Lady Lyell, and to Lyell, too, and good orthodox mince pies to celebrate it with. How many of your countrymen, by the by, are indebted to Washington Irving for showing the world what a beautiful thing Christmas is, or used to be, in your brave little island. I was reading his account of it this morning, stuffed as full of racy old English rhymes as Christmas pudding is of plums. It is odd that a book like this, so finely and delicately executed, should come from the New World, where one expects to meet with hardly anything more than the raw material. It has been a quiet winter, quiet in every sense, for the old greybeard has not ventured to shake his hoary locks at us yet, or at least has shed none of them on the ground, which is as bare as November. But winter is not likely to rot in the sky, and we shall soon see the feathers dancing about us.*

The week of Christmas had always been a time of particular satisfaction for him, as much when he was a child as when he had his own family. In the shops, as November approached December, the change could be seen. Barrels of candy were rolled in between the bags of sugar, and toys were suspended from the ceiling with the other wares. In wooden boxes lined with red paper and filled with sawdust and shavings, their contents ruffled into a seductive state of confusion, were the firecrackers, torpedoes, and Roman candles. The season brought a succession of other luxuries: English walnuts, Brazil nuts, Malaga grapes, delicacies available at no other time of year. An exotic treat for the family was the coconut; for a dime it opened a world of unusual taste. The milk was dripped through a hole in one of the eyes, and the meat grated for pies, and a cake thickly filled with coconut would be enough to keep Christmas a happy memory for many years. It was in the Christmas season that we first learned there was such a fruit as the orange. There were sweets made with its peelings and baked into tight, hard loafs to be savoured over the week. A cinnamon stick rubbed around the house would give off the smell of cinnamon, and a syrup of cinnamon, cloves, and oranges would be boiled up with a bit of rum to be served with the Christmas loaf. Around this time of the year, Prescott's mother and father would gather the figs their cousin Adam had brought from the South and would take them when they went visiting, wrapped in wax paper and tied with a glittering silver ribbon. His mother would pull from their storage room all the Christmas decorations, children playing in the snow, horses pulling sleighs, golden bells tied with long red ribbon, and the garlands and the mistletoe, and on the twenty-first of December they would decorate the house and would hang the ornaments on the tree — real fruit embellished with gold leaf, little drummer men, tiny chairs and beds and cupboards, as if for a miniature house. Their Christmas week was so full of obligations and social engagements that, as a grown man, Prescott once joked that he was a drinker as his father had been, but only for one week out of the year. The city was always lit up with candles — even the trees in the law offices were decorated, and on city streets, wreaths decorated with holly berries ornamented the doorways on all sides. I was taken into their home during the festive season. As children, we were allowed to fill the green and red tarlatan bags with hard candies, and as soon as I was old enough, it was my special delight to fill two bowls of the best china with newly whipped cream. In the early days of Prescott's marriage to Claire, she would dress herself in a long velvet gown, her hair pulled back, her eyes glistening with the excitement of the week, moving giddily from one party to the next, into the cold night, escaping inside a hot parlour and taking a ladle of strong eggnog. They played billiards, drank wine, played cards, sleighed and skated on the ice, enjoyed repeated sessions of wild goose, partridge, spareribs, tongue and udder, turkey and oysters, venison pastry, minced mutton, mutton stew, boiled pigeon and bacon, and assorted other combinations. From the cellar came jams and jellies, and from the kitchen came the smell of rich, cream-filled, fruit-filled loafs and thickly packed pies, mellowed spirits and sharp spices and crystallized fruits and breads, still warm and puffed from their pans.

Two p.m. brought dinner with well-cured Virginia hams, pork and beef, fish, duck, a superb turkey and gravy. There were hot chocolate and rolls after three by the shimmering sight of the tree, and in the washhouse copper, hot apples would be hissing and bubbling with a rich look and a jolly sound that were perfectly irresistible.

Whether I am invited again or no, I will always honour Christmas in my heart and try to keep it all the year.

ONLY CLAIRE WAS PERMITTED to stay with Prescott during his final days, not Bentham, not Amory, and not myself. Not even Mr. Gardiner was given entrance, and while many condemned the nurse for her unfeelingness, it was the desire of the entire family that Prescott not be subjected to the pain of his associates in his final days, his own pain being great enough. Still, no one could bear to think that the next occasion of their meeting would be at his funeral, which, it was clear, would be attended by everyone who had ever made his acquaintance. That his funeral would be a social function of the sort he had hosted all his life should not have been a surprise, but for those closest to him, to have to share the day with those who knew him less well and loved him less, was a sign that there had only ever been Claire in his heart, and not his friends, who were perhaps so many social ornaments, more like the jewellery on the hands of one so admired than intimates at all.

The sky was still light, and when I rushed down Cedar Street my hat fell off and blew in the warm breeze down the road. I had set out quickly in a determined way, though the night had just begun and my suit was damp with sweat. Still, there was no thought in me of going back as I hurried on through the streets.

Prescott had written to have me celebrate with him the publication of his *Peru*, in a banquet hall with supper, which I was eager to attend. He had said in the invitation that he did not believe that the scholars in the public would be in the least pleased with this sort of festivity, so it gave him immense delight to give it. That evening, the gently lit hall was thick with the fumes of cigars, and at each table was a centrepiece of white and purple grapes that were mammoth, and cut-glass jars in which a peculiar arrangement of flowers and fruit gave a joyous air, as though for the celebration of a marriage or birth and not a book of history. Prescott finished his speech and, smiling, told us to enjoy the night, that he hoped we liked the game — after which there was large and approving laughter from one of the tables across the room, the reason for which I did not understand. The people I was seated with were an unremarkable bunch, and not one among them was in a position to help me — a sombre cripple, cousins of Claire from outside of Boston, a retired old man called Lord E_it with his two sons, one a student of the law and the other in the Navy. *We lead a very rational way of life*, the old man said to me at one point. Finally I made to excuse myself and stepped out into the lobby where the smell of fumes was the strongest and where I hoped that I might, if I lingered long enough, be taken into a conversation, but when I stepped into the lobby, glittering so brightly from the chandeliers all up and down it, there was only Addison with the editor of the *North American Review*, both of them leaning against the wall and smoking. Addison, catching sight of me before the great doors had even closed behind me, did not let a moment pass before he said out loud, looking straight at me, *Watch yourself, George*, then gripped his friend by the arm and pulled him away from me down the hall, while I stood there, unable to move, the wine glass now quivering in my hand. I set it down carefully on the little side table I was standing near, and felt my stomach clutch and my bowels nearly give way. Not knowing where to go, and not even thinking of returning to my seat to get Prescott's book, which I had purchased earlier that night, I found my way to the front doors, heavy, pushed on them hard, and left.

I ALONE, PERHAPS, AM best able to chart the progression, from the start of his infirmity when he was still young and we were boyhood friends. Among the modes he adopted at the time to regulate his conduct was one that had far more effect on him later in life than it did when I returned for the holidays, not eager to see my family. When you visited him at his home on Summer Street, you noticed a change in him. There was no resemblance to the schoolboy he'd been before, and this set him apart, this manner you had not known could come from a boy of your age. He had no visible sorrow over his own condition and said nothing about it, except to answer questions about his health in a res-olute but slightly impatient way. Then you lost your old habit of conversing and did not know what to say, sit-ting there before him, ashamed and tired. He had taken on no sign of bitterness but had lost all the romantic illusions we once had shared, and the manner he adopt-ed was of one who might sit alone for any length of time, and I felt there was no place for me in what his life had become.

I had been in the hall when it struck the open eye — a rare occurrence in the case of that vigilant organ. You had been at the other end of the room, when you looked up in time to see him fall and the others rush around. He had turned his head at the call of his name from any one of the hundreds of boys on dozens of benches eating the ends of their lunch, but the bread roll was not aimed at him, crusty and hard. There had been many classmates jumping about him in the general excitement at the end of the hour when we all were try-ing to leave. He was almost out the door, and had his name not been called and had he not quickly turned to acknowledge it, he would not have been laid up swollen and bleeding and out of exams for six months, lying in the parlour of the house of his mother and father, miles from school, covered in the pleated quilt I saw when I returned, waiting in the dark with his polite but quiet pose that demanded no comfort, a behaviour he fell into after the accident, developing those qualities which have worked to make him the man he is now, and have assured his success both here and across the Atlantic. That the calamity befell him in the freshness of his youth cannot be overlooked. The bread roll went straight into the open eye and the force of it toppled him so he lay flat and bleeding while everyone crowded around, a whole din-ing hall of boys in blue pants and blazers peering into his face, and after he was carried off we still stood about. I stood there the longest. No, you did not. You returned, like the others, to your lunch. It had been the usual gaiety only moments before, and the bread had certainly been launched at random. It had come from the hand of any one of the dozens of boys who were jumping about and throwing things in the eruption at the end of the hour, once the older boys had already left. *It punctured the eye*, they told us as we sat in our desks. *It has punctured the eye and we won't see him for the rest of the term, perhaps not until next year*. There was a quietness as we considered the gravity of missing so much school.

When I went to visit over the Christmas holidays with my mother and father, he sat in the darkened room with the quilt laid over his legs and chest and did not talk of his own condition, and did not ask about our friends. His conduct had changed and the mode he adopted to regulate himself seemed not to have come from the boy he had been before. His yellowish face frightened me. You looked away. I did not know what to say to those qualities that had once made him thrilling but now made him strange. I left the parlour and went obediently and readily home with my mother and father. It was not only myself but also his parents who were uneasy with the suddenness of having a new man in the house. As for the careful examination I made at his request, of both the damaged eye and his regular one, I could see nothing but the inner floating of a whitish haze attached to nothing, which he already knew about, he told me with exasperation, pushing away my hand.

Returning that January to school I found frost in the grass, whispering boys, and a new book-master in the dorm. And while after two weeks no one spoke of Prescott at all, I could not forget him sitting in his parents' house, or having gone to visit him in the parlour, so dark I couldn't have called it day. I listened patiently to all he had worked out, beginning to end, and what he believed of the boy who had thrown the bread. For him there was no blame, only acceptance; a Christian act that impressed me deeply, for no one ever apologized. And although the blow had certainly been given by accident, the one who had thrown the bread roll never expressed any sympathy for Prescott's terrible loss. At least, the sufferer, to whom, if anyone, he should have expressed it, never knew that he regretted what he had done.

When Mary fled for Paris she did so without telling Prescott, though I long knew what she had been planning — but she refused to inform Prescott, stating that whatever his reaction, it would serve only to frustrate what she had been looking forward to, without pleasure, as the solution to her life in Boston, where she had been living with her half-brother and his young wife. It was that the charity Prescott had forgotten to extend or failed to extend to her a third time around made it too shameful for her to call on him again, and so she did not, and wrote him only two or three letters more before she disappeared; the last a heavy, folded sheet of paper to which a pin had been applied, the letters pricked out so he could read it by himself, perhaps forgiving him, perhaps knowing that the world of the blind is so circumscribed by the little circle they can span with their arms.

The day was dark when I went home, making my way through the streets like a man who's lost nothing. Before the funeral there had been a wash and a shave, and I sat in the noisy church among the hundreds who had come to bid him farewell, some knowing him well, some not at all — readers, editors, and all manner of important personages. Those closest to him carried his coffin on their shoulders through the mud-soaked streets, and I followed at a distance, in the midst of the crowd, shoved on all sides by those who wanted to get a better look at what remained of the man they perhaps had spoken to only once in his long life. Not far ahead of me I spotted her black cap and the thin line of her jaw. She was walking unaccompanied and looking straight ahead, and I grew certain that I had never felt anything against his fine nurse. I had understood that she had so much been working for his own interest, not the interest of his friends, and that while for this reason we had been excluded from his final days and weeks, it was only with the intention of putting Prescott in the best spirits, as the friends and families of the ailing often ask so much of the sufferer. It had been the rest — Mr. Gardiner, Addison, Bentham — who made the fuss and created the crisis in those final weeks as they sought to have her returned to England, claiming she was acting against the desires of Prescott and in the selfish interest of Claire alone, and they did succeed, for several days, in creating the impression that she would be sent home and replaced by the doughy, complacent, and ineffectual nurse who had been his caregiver in the early years of his illness; a kind but scattered woman who did him little service and allowed him to be visited any moment of the day and night. You allowed yourself to be kept away. I did not try to force my way into his house in the final weeks, in the manner of Bentham and Gardiner and the rest, who believed it was Prescott's desire because it was theirs. It was only the English nurse who stood in the way of their seeing Prescott in his final days, holding fast to her resolve to the end, and the next time his friends were allowed near him was on the day of his burial. After the funeral she returned to her work at the Asylum for the Blind, but within several weeks they succeeded in returning her to England. The Asylum picked a nurse from the lower ranks to assume her role, and his friends felt much vindicated by this final gesture, imagining that Prescott was thanking them from his grave. But I no longer spoke to any of Prescott's friends following his death, and could not say whether Claire had any regret over their behaviour, or was too consumed by her loss to have noticed it at all.

IN ALL, OF ALL THE GREAT sorrows that marked the day of his passing, none was so great as mine, none so carefully tuned to the harmony of his own life, which had shrouded me since we were boys; the light of his glories, his affection for his family, and the generosity and love of learning that so occupied his mind. My whole body ached with remorse and suffering at the extinguishing of a flame that had burned so brightly, brighter than any I had ever known. Nothing had so filled my heart as my dear friend Prescott, to whom I shall forever be indebted, and should I die, I pray I do it with even a measure of the grace that he did, smiling to the last, with no fear, only that moral courage I so often longed would be mine.

III

I told myself I'd take a bath, prepare myself as I had before. I tell myself that evening-time is when my life comes alive, but that is not true either. Instead I left. Now I walk through the streets with my head hung low, the flowers dragging from my hand. I push them under a pile of leaves to hide them from the rain. There isn't any hope or even a thought in me of going back while everything around me is calling out my guilt as I pass by; the streetcar lines, the chimney stacks, that storefront on the corner with the fruit in bins, the streetlights and the wires hanging overhead. But what has been the cause this time? Why has it turned out the way it has? I'd been, so late in the day, quite certain of the success that would come, and like a fool I'd pulled my suit from the floor and hung it over the edge of the bathtub to dry, early in the afternoon, a feeling of hope still in me like spring. But it's impossible to think I didn't foresee it — staring up at the warmly lit windows from the street, softly holding the coins in my pocket, and wishing I was inside already. I stood there like a beggar, then turned and left through the rain-soaked streets. The whole afternoon had involved nothing more than dressing up, a wash, and a shave, and when I looked in the mirror I thought I'd at last met a man to be proud of. I had played myself talking easily, complimenting myself on my genius like an actor preparing his lines. I imagined I'd be like the rest, standing around with a drink in my hand, important words and laughter all about my head. But I was far from the centre of it all, a miniature down in the street, and looking up at the window I saw the well-dressed women, and Amory by the drapes, flirting with a woman dressed in beads and pearls. What is the point in pretending now? The world is as foursquare as my room. I left their walk and pulled myself through the rain-dark streets, so lost I forgot my name. When at last I looked up I found it all impassive and I stopped. There was no looking at me, not by the trees or the houses or the streetlamps; nothing about them was calling out my guilt as I passed by. I can see the bicycles tied to the poles and the drooping awnings and my soiled shoes. There is a light from the grocery window on the corner, shining into the street, and so many blocks still to walk, but even as I leave, from the window's light there is no disapproval at all. Then I move through the streets proudly, like a man who's loved nothing. Finally I come upon a restaurant, warm inside and serving food from a grill, and entering, I sit along the counter, slightly trembling, fumbling for a newspaper. *You'll be happy, you'll see*, people used to tease. But ten years of effort have resulted in ten years of effort and the same place to stand in. I'd caught glimpses of glory that I would not share, and for weeks I'd thought sixteen, eighteen hours a day, without fatigue, in my room. Standing up I find myself shaking, then go into the road for a taxi. The driver says nothing as I gaze out at the rain-soaked streets, though no rain has fallen for hours. Calmly then, nothing impedes my breathing. There is no new sediment before my eyes. When I step into my room, the rosiness at the moment I enter softens me some. The light is on and everything in it acknowledges my arrival, everything laid out as I know it best, the books and papers — their placement is very true to time — a billfold, an umbrella, two jackets discarded carelessly, and the cups and plates I had left about. A new state has gone up in me. I feel it there, so light on the floor I forget my feet. Outside no one speaks, no one moves, the moon can be seen fully from the window and it lights up a patch on the floor. I become quiet and I pray. I find myself looking forward to this time as I look forward to some events, dear God, like the coming of summer. I see how splendid life is and how many responsibilities I have. Tomorrow, when I wake to the bright day, things will run as smoothly as a machine and I will live.

Author's Note

Ticknor was inspired by *The Life of William Hickling Prescott* by George Ticknor (Philadelphia, PA: J. B. Lippincott Company, 1863). Certain phrases have been borrowed from that book, and from the work of other writers, including Florence Nightingale, Marie Stopes, and Sofia Tolstoy.